PRAISE FOR *AFTER THE RED CARPET*

"Leavy's novels invite you into a world of love and romance like no other. *After the Red Carpet* is a charming, tender, smart, and thought-provoking story about how to maintain personal autonomy after love and marriage. This gorgeous book is so cozy and satisfying, it's like being wrapped in a hug. The ending will make you believe in happily ever after. Highly recommend!"
—Jessie Voigts, PhD, founder of Wandering Educators

"Leavy, an acclaimed romance novelist, brings us a brave, emotionally charged, and deceptively subtle story about the intensity of love and the complexity of forging a new world for oneself. This is both a deeply beautiful love story for the ages and a smart exploration of what happens to our identities when 'me' becomes 'we.' I could not put this book down. The ending is everything."
—Jessica Smartt Gullion, author of *October Birds*

"*After the Red Carpet* offers a brilliant spin on a Cinderella story that is equal parts whimsical fairy tale and insightful meditation on the true meaning of love. Ella and Finn show us that happily ever after is possible once you let go of the fairy tale and your fears, and that the greatest gift is simply loving someone for who they really are. Readers of women's fiction and romance novels will devour this book. The ending is supremely satisfying."
—U. Melissa Anyiwo, editor of *Gender Warriors*

PRAISE FOR *THE LOCATION SHOOT*

"Each character is more charming than the next . . .
the intellectual discussions throughout the book prove
fresh and engaging and will keep the pages turning. A
quick-witted depiction of moviemaking best suited for
contemplative romantics."

—*Kirkus Reviews*

"Patricia Leavy's *The Location Shoot* is hard to put down.
. . . Leavy is a master storyteller, skillfully weaving
together a narrative that keeps us engaged from start
to finish. . . . Ultimately, it's a must-read for anyone
looking for a thought-provoking and entertaining
exploration of love, relationships, and self-discovery.
Highly recommended!"

—*Readers' Favorite*, 5-star review

"The narrative's charm isn't solely defined by the romantic
entanglement of a central couple but also by its well-
sketched ensemble cast."

—Literary Titan, 5-star review

"A tour de force! Much more than a romance, this novel
celebrates the romance of life itself. Leavy's voice in fiction
is singular. She brings her laser-like wit, intelligence, and
hopefulness to this enchanting and truly unforgettable
love story."

—Laurel Richardson, author of *Lone Twin*

PRAISE FOR *HOLLYLAND*

"This quick read will leave readers satisfied with the happy ending. The main characters will make readers believe in love. Fans of Colleen Hoover and Tessa Bailey will enjoy *Hollyland*."
　　　　　　　　—Booklist

"Some fun secondary characters, a well-drawn setting, and an exciting eleventh-hour kidnapping plot propel Leavy's story."
　　　　　　　　—Kirkus Reviews

". . . Leavy weaves a lot of excitement, charm, and romance into this concise and highly engrossing novel . . . Overall, I would not hesitate to recommend *Hollyland* to fans of romance and women's fiction everywhere; you will not be disappointed."
　　　　　　　—Readers' Favorite, 5-star review

"Written with the kind of eloquence associated with award winning literary fiction . . . An impressively poignant, laudably original, and thoroughly entertaining novel that moves fluidly between romance, humor, suspense, and joy, *Hollyland* is one of those stories that will linger in the mind and memory long after the book itself has been finished and set back upon the shelf . . . highly recommended."
　　　　　　　　—Midwest Book Review

AFTER THE RED CARPET

AFTER THE
RED
CARPET

A NOVEL

PATRICIA LEAVY

SHE WRITES PRESS

Published 2024
Printed in the United States of America
Print ISBN: 978-1-64742-750-4
E-ISBN: 978-1-64742-751-1
Library of Congress Control Number: 2024903207

For information, address:
She Writes Press
1569 Solano Ave #546
Berkeley, CA 94707

Interior Design by Tabitha Lahr

She Writes Press is a division of SparkPoint Studio, LLC.

For Mark Robins

PROLOGUE

May 21   *Entertainment News Report*

The last day of the Cannes Film Festival proved to be the stuff of legend. We all thought the big story would be the highly anticipated screening of Jean Mercier's latest film, *Celebration*, which featured Albie Hughes's final performance, but in fact, it was Finn Forrester who stole the show. Captivating the world and igniting a feeding frenzy among the press and onlookers, the Hollywood star got down on bended knee in the center of the famed red carpet and proposed to writer Gabriella Sinclair, known for her provocative philosophical musings on sexual politics. The huge rock he slid onto her finger was almost as blinding as the incredible firestorm of camera flashes his proposal generated, the likes of which we've never before seen. When Finn picked up his bride-to-be, spun her around, and kissed her passionately, it was clear she had said yes. Rumor has it that Sinclair is a longtime friend of Mercier, and the pair reportedly met on the location shoot for the film.

While Forrester's many fans took to social media to share a collective sigh, bemoaning the fact that the beloved leading man is officially off the market, many others gushed at the iconic fairy-tale moment. Costars were quick to add their congratulations. Willow Barnes retweeted a photo of the pair kissing on the red carpet with the caption "Aww . . . I always said you two made the cutest couple ever," followed by a string of heart emojis. Charlotte Reed commented, "Feeling warm and fuzzy. Couldn't be happier for you both," and Michael Hennesey wrote, "Way to go, guys! Let's meet for a drink in LA." When Mercier was asked if the proposal seen around the world was a publicity stunt, the tempestuous director laughed and said, "I'm not that clever. I'm thrilled for my friends, who are very much in love. I wish them a lifetime of happiness." The reporter then asked if Mercier was worried the engagement would steal the spotlight away from his film, to which he replied, "You're talking about it, so no." Forrester and Sinclair made a quick exit after the film screening, avoiding detection. One thing is for sure: the world will be watching, waiting to see how this real-life fairy tale unfolds after the red carpet.

 **CHAPTER 1**

Ella woke up, her naked body cradled in Finn's strong embrace. She noticed the sun peering through the hotel window shades, wondered what time it was, and lightly touched his hand.

"Good morning, sweetheart," he said, squeezing her.

"Good morning, my love," she replied, turning to face him.

He gently ran his finger from her brow to her cheekbone. "God, it feels so good to wake up with you."

"I was afraid to fall asleep, afraid that I'd wake up and discover it was all a dream."

He rested his hand on her cheek and kissed her forehead. "Me too. But it's real, baby. We're finally back together, the way we're meant to be."

She started to smile, but it morphed into a yawn.

Finn laughed and said, "I guess I should have let you get more sleep last night. I just couldn't get enough of you."

"Yes, you had quite the voracious appetite. Seems you really missed sex."

"I missed sex with *you*. The truth is, I missed everything with you, Ella."

"Me too. Besides, I wouldn't trade a night of making love with you over and over again for anything," she said.

"Hold that thought, because I'm not done with you yet," he replied, skimming her hand and slipping out of bed. "I'm going to brush my teeth, and then I'll be back to ravage you again."

"You really are the sexiest man I've ever seen," she remarked, staring at his sculpted, naked body. "I missed watching you walk away almost as much as I missed watching you walk toward me."

"Don't you move."

A few minutes later, Finn emerged with minty-fresh breath. Ella hopped out of bed and said, "My turn."

He grazed her arm as she passed. "There's an extra toothbrush on the counter."

When Ella returned, Finn was standing outside the bathroom waiting for her. She smiled coyly, and he took her hand and pulled her to him. He swept her long curls back and started kissing her ear, working his way to her neck and then her mouth. He turned her around, wrapped one arm around her, and traced the curves of her body with his other hand. When he touched between her legs, she writhed and moaned with delight. "That's it, baby," he whispered, nibbling on her earlobe. She leaned forward, resting her hands on a chair, and softly commanded, "Take me."

He slid inside her, moving slowly as they both let out small groans. "Oh, God. I need you, Finn," she whimpered. He began intensely pounding until they both screamed in bliss.

"I love you so much, Ella," he whispered as he tried to catch his breath, their quivering bodies pressed together.

"I love you too, body and soul," she said in return.

He kissed her bare shoulder, took her hand, and said, "Come snuggle me."

They crawled into bed and exchanged tender kisses, running their fingers through each other's hair.

"I've never been happier," he said.

2

"Me too," she replied, outstretching her hand and admiring the huge, sparkling engagement ring on her finger.

"Do you like the ring?" he asked. "They told me the oval cut was the most romantic."

"It's incredible. I love it because it's from you." She paused. "Finn, what's going to happen now?"

"Now we're going to live happily ever after."

She smiled. "I know, but . . ."

"What, baby?"

"Well, right now, we're in Cannes. My things are in my apartment in Paris. We're moving to your place in LA. I guess I'm just wondering how this will work and what's going to happen next. I feel a little adrift. This is all new to me."

He cupped her cheek. "It's new to me too, but don't worry; we'll figure everything out together. We're partners now, in everything, always." She smiled and he continued, "This afternoon, the awards will be announced at the festival's closing ceremony. Then there'll be a press conference. I'm supposed to join Jean and the others for a press panel on *Celebration*, but I'm sure they'll understand if I don't make it."

"No, my love. Go to the ceremony and press conference. Support your beautiful film. Maybe I can hide in the back somewhere, and then we can catch up with everyone afterward."

"After today, my work here is done. In two weeks, I'm scheduled for a string of publicity obligations in LA, which will take a few days. Then I have some voice-over work to do, also in LA, followed by more press stuff. My next film doesn't start shooting until the middle of July. It's filming on location in Boston, and I was hoping you'd join me."

"I would love that," Ella said.

"What about you? Have you finished your big project on pleasure? Is there anywhere you need to be this summer?"

"The only place I need to be is with you. Yes, I finished all four books. Delivered them to my publisher last week, as

3

a matter of fact. When they're released, I'll need to schedule a small book tour. Maybe you can tag along."

"Absolutely. We'll make it work," Finn assured her. "What's next for you?"

"I need to develop my next project. I'm not quite sure what it'll be yet, but I want it to be something I can really sink my teeth into. I'm still chasing the big questions." She giggled. "But one of the greatest things about my work is that I can do it anywhere."

"So, we have two weeks coming up with no obligations, no demands. How should we spend them? We could stay here, soaking up the Riviera. Then we could take my jet to Paris to pack up your things and head to LA, or we could just send for your things. If you'd rather spend some time in Paris to see your friends or whatever, we could head straight there. For that matter, we could fly straight to LA if you'd like some time to get settled in before I have to work." He planted a delicate kiss on the tip of her nose and stroked her cheek. "And if you don't like any of those ideas, just tell me what works for you, baby. All I want is to make you happy."

She smiled. "Finn, I'm ready to start our life together. It would be nice to have some time to get settled into your house before you're busy. Why don't we spend a couple of days here, and then we can fly to LA? I have a neighbor with a key to my apartment; I'm sure she can pack my things for me if you can have them shipped. I don't have very much."

"I'll take care of everything."

"My kitten, Sweden, is in my room. I'll need to go check on her soon. I guess I'll grab my suitcase and just move in here. I don't want to be apart for even a minute." She looked around and ogled Finn's massive suite. "This place really is extraordinary. I barely noticed it last night after we raced down the hallway like wild teenagers. I don't know what came over me; I guess I just couldn't wait another moment to be alone with you."

"Well, you got the nicer room at the inn during the shoot. When I made the reservation, I made sure to get the best room they had. I was hoping we'd be sharing it."

"You were?"

He nodded and she lightly pressed her mouth to his.

"Should we order up some room service? We left the after-party so quickly last night that we never ate a thing. I'm just now realizing how hungry I am," he said.

"Oh, that reminds me. I don't know if I ever told you how marvelous the film is. It really leaves one pondering the big questions. Your performance was gorgeous; you should be tremendously proud. And for you all to receive a standing ovation must have made you feel good."

"I was distracted by how good it felt to have you by my side," he replied, kissing her bare shoulder. "I should probably see what the papers have to say so I don't stumble into the press conference unprepared. Why don't you take a look at that menu over there?" he suggested, gesturing to her nightstand. "I'll throw on a robe and see if the newspapers have been delivered."

"Okay, but kiss me first."

He smiled and kissed her passionately before hopping out of bed and slipping into a robe. He retrieved a matching robe from the closet, handed it to her, and went to check outside the room. Ella put on the lush garment and grabbed the room service menu. "Sweetheart," Finn said, walking back to her, holding a stack of newspapers and looking slightly dazed.

"Good reviews?" she asked, raising her eyebrows.

"Yeah, of our engagement. We're on the front page of every newspaper around the world."

# CHAPTER 2

"**Y**ou've been gazing out the window for most of the flight. What are you daydreaming about?" Finn asked, draping his arm around Ella.

She turned to look at him and smiled softly. "Nothing, really. Just watching the clouds beneath us."

He pecked her lips.

"What about you?" she asked. "You must be on cloud nine yourself with the incredible response to the film. Winning the Palme d'Or, the biggest award of the festival. It's extraordinary."

He smiled. "I only wish Albie had been there to celebrate with us all."

"Me too. Although he once told me that he found awards to be a bit preposterous. He called them 'dust collectors for the chronically insecure,' which cracked me up." They both laughed and Ella continued, "Making good art and living with gusto both on- and off-screen—that's what mattered to him. And that's what the film captures."

"Yeah."

"Jean, on the other hand, no doubt derived great personal satisfaction from the win. For years he's felt so misunderstood, attacked by the mainstream media. They've relished

7

labeling him controversial. To be fair, he's certainly gone out of his way to play it up, to have fun with the absurdity. I caught his eye when the award was announced, and I could tell he was having a good giggle at it all." She paused and touched his face. "I'm honored to have been there when you were all making such a spectacular piece of art. You truly deserve the accolades."

"Ella, this film changed my life in every way. It will always be the most special shoot of my life because it's where we met and fell in love. The reception the film is receiving is just the icing on the cake. To tell you the truth, I haven't given the award or the recognition a single thought. I've been too preoccupied by thinking about how happy I am that we're together."

She leaned forward and pressed her lips to his. "I should really take little Sweden out of her travel carrier."

"I'll get her," Finn replied, bending over and retrieving the small kitten. "Hi, sweet little thing," he said, gently petting her snow-white fur. "Here you go. She's trembling."

Ella took her carefully. "Oh, it's okay, little one. This is an adventure, that's all."

"Is she all right?" Finn asked.

"I think she's just a little nervous."

"Are you nervous too, sweetheart? It's okay if you are. Leaving Paris and your friends, moving to LA, being thrust into the spotlight . . . it's a lot."

She looked deeply into his sea-colored eyes and said, "Losing you was the most painful thing I've ever been through."

"It was for me too."

"When we fell in love and you started talking about our future, so often there were things I was thinking, things I wanted to say, but I didn't because I was afraid of hurting you or disappointing you somehow. So instead, I let things fester, tried to bury them, until I had retreated so far into myself that I didn't know how to tell you what I was feeling. I barely knew what I was feeling myself."

"You can tell me anything, Ella."

"I know that now. I promised myself a long time ago that if I were ever lucky enough to get another chance with you, I wouldn't make those same mistakes again. Finn, I want us to share everything, to be real partners, like you said."

He played with one of her curls, waiting to hear what she would say next.

"So, to answer your question, I'm mostly out-of-my-mind excited for everything that's ahead. But yes, I'm also a tad nervous. This is all new to me—moving in with someone, building a life together." She glanced down. He touched her cheek, and she raised her gaze to meet his. "Leaving my home for yours isn't hard. I've always looked at taking leaps as a part of the adventure of life, and I love LA. It's just . . ."

"What, baby?"

"You live in a mansion. You have a staff. That's so wildly different from what I'm used to that it's hard to wrap my mind around it. I don't know what to expect or how I'll fit into your world."

"Sweetheart, I promise to do everything in my power to make you comfortable. When we get to the house tonight, it will be empty. I thought we could use privacy, and I didn't want to overwhelm you. I gave the staff the day off tomorrow so the two of us can unwind. We can just take it day by day. The details will sort themselves out. Remember, it won't be *my* world or *my* home anymore; it will be ours. Nothing is set in stone. If something makes you uncomfortable, we can change it. We'll figure out what works for us."

"That means a lot to me," she said before planting a soft kiss on his mouth.

"Ella, all I want is for us to be together and live the life we've dreamed of."

"The last time around, I think we suffered from feeling pressure, confusion, or doubt, not trusting that our feelings were mutual. Maybe we didn't know in our hearts that we belonged to each other. This time, I want to make sure you know that, and that you know I do too."

Warmth swept over his face.

"Finn, there's something I need you to know and remember, something you can trust in the deepest part of your soul. It will help take the pressure off so I don't need to worry about being flawless, living up to a fantasy, or always saying or doing the perfect thing."

"What, baby?"

"I choose you. I choose us. Always."

WHEN THE JET LANDED, A TOWN CAR was waiting to whisk them home. Ella held Sweden's carrier on her lap as they drove through the most exclusive part of Beverly Hills. "We're here," Finn announced as the gates opened. "It's just up this private drive."

"Wow," Ella muttered, wide-eyed as they pulled up to the front of the circular driveway, a fountain in the center. She'd seen photos of his house, but it was somehow even grander in person.

She stepped hesitantly out of the car, while Finn spilled out with the confidence of coming home. "Wait here. Let me unlock the door and turn off the alarm. The driver can run the luggage upstairs. He can take Sweden too," Finn instructed, taking the pet carrier. "I want us to walk inside together."

Ella nodded and the men set off on their tasks. She waited, breathing in the crisp night air and admiring the imposing gray house with white trim and mammoth windows, surrounded by perfectly manicured plants and flowers. Finn returned and took her hand. "Come on, my love," he said. As they stepped into the foyer, Ella's eyes flitted from the dark wood floors to the light gray walls, massively high ceilings, and grand, spiral staircase. "Welcome home, sweetheart."

She beamed. "It's amazing."

"Are you hungry? I'm sure that Joyce, my cook, loaded the fridge for us."

She shook her head. "I'm still full from the food on the flight. But if you're hungry . . ."

"I'm not. Would you like a tour?"

"It's kind of a lot to take in all at once. I'm trying to stay grounded by focusing only on you. Maybe we could go to your bedroom and save the tour for tomorrow—is that okay?"

"Of course. It's just upstairs," he replied, showing her the way. When they arrived at the open door, he said, "After you, my love."

She stepped into the sprawling bedroom, immediately noticing the tiered crystal chandelier hanging high above. She mumbled, "Oh, wow," a smile dancing across her face. "It's nothing like I imagined. I thought it might be, well . . ."

"What?" he asked.

"A bachelor on his own and all, I guess I assumed it would be hypermasculine. But if I were going to fantasize about the most dreamlike, serene bedroom, this would be it. The furniture is gorgeous," she said, admiring the walnut bed frame with mother-of-pearl inlay. "This must feel like sleeping on a cloud," she remarked, running her hand across the silvery-gray sateen comforter. "Oh, and this vanity and love seat are absolutely beautiful, like out of a fairy tale. I've never had anything like this before. Oh, and look here! These are so lovely," she gushed, meandering over to a table by the windows and picking up a small vase filled with pale pink rosebuds. "They smell so sweet."

He smiled brightly. "I'm so glad you like it. It's all new. For you, Ella."

"What?" she asked, raising her eyebrows in surprise.

"This has all been done in the last two days. My decorator took care of everything. She's been working around the clock, texting me pictures so I could approve each item. I wanted our home to be perfect for you, especially this room. I hope it can be a sanctuary, an oasis."

Her eyes became misty. "You did all of this for me?"

He caressed the side of her face and nodded.

"It's like something out of a fantasy. How did you possibly . . ."

"I know you, Ella. I told her that you love things with history but that you're also the most modern person I know. I insisted that nothing should ever be brought into this house that doesn't have romance to it, because that's how you make me feel." He wiped a tear that had fallen from her eye and continued, "The furniture is art deco inspired. Since that style originated in France and you left Paris to move here with me, I thought it would be a nice way to merge our worlds. We chose this bedding because I could picture you lying on it. I could visualize just how piercing your green eyes would look against the cool gray."

"Finn, I don't know what to say," she said with a sniffle.

"You don't have to say anything. I promised that when you moved here, it wouldn't be my world; it would be ours. There may be all kinds of changes you want to make around here to make it feel like home, but I wanted to get a head start."

"You are the sweetest, most romantic man I've ever known," she said, taking his face in her hands and kissing him softly. "Oh, and look! You even got little Sweden a kitty bed."

"There are a few scattered throughout the house. They said this was the softest, most lush kind. There are also bowls set up for her."

She ran her hand down his bicep and pulled him close. He wrapped her in his muscular arms. "Thank you," she whispered.

He dropped a kiss in her hair. "You are so welcome." After a moment, he asked, "Should we unpack and get ready for bed?"

"That sounds divine."

"Here's our closet," he said, leading her into an enormous walk-in with rows of built-in clothing racks, shoe racks, drawers, and mirrors. Three round white ottomans filled the center of the monstrous space.

She laughed and remarked, "This is literally bigger than my last apartment."

"My things are on that side over there, and I've cleared out the rest for you. It will be a couple of days before your belongings arrive from Paris, so I asked my assistant to pick up a few things for you: robes, pajamas, jeans, tops, the long sundresses you love, workout clothes, bathing suits, and a few pairs of sandals and sneakers. There should be underwear and socks in one of these drawers," he said, opening several. "Ah, here they are."

"Finn, I . . . I . . ."

"What, baby?"

"I just can't believe you did all of this. You didn't have to go to such trouble. The only thing I need is you."

"It was no trouble. It's just a few things to make you more comfortable and at home. Of course, if there's anything else you need, we can buy it. There are toiletries in the bathroom. I think I remembered everything you use, your face wash, lotion, toothpaste, perfume."

She ran her hand down the light teal silk robe hanging in the closet, which had been picked out for her. When she turned back to him, she said in a sultry voice, "Let's get ready for bed. I want to feel you."

A little while later, Ella emerged from the bathroom wearing her new robe, her long, spiral curls flowing freely. Finn skimmed his fingertips across her wrist, and then onto her cheek. They began kissing tenderly and with increasing intensity. She untied the sash to her robe and let it fall to the floor.

"My God, you're beautiful. I think it every time I'm with you like this," he said.

She slipped her fingers under his waistband and pulled his boxer shorts down, stopping at the indentation above his tailbone. Running her hands down his muscular thighs, she fell to her knees and took him in her mouth. He moaned with pleasure. When he couldn't take it anymore, he helped her rise to her feet, picked her up, and carefully laid her down on the bed. They made love intimately, kissing each other until they both groaned in ecstasy.

"I'm completely in love with you and I always will be," Finn whispered, staring at her in total adoration.

"And I'm completely in love with you. Finn, I'm so happy to be here."

He kissed her forehead, reached over to switch off the light, and then scooped her up in his arms. "Welcome home, sweetheart."

 CHAPTER 3

"**M**mm, I was right. It was like sleeping on a cloud," Ella said as she stretched and turned to face Finn.

"Good morning, my love," he said as he pulled her body against his.

"What time is it?"

He craned his neck to look at the clock. "A little after nine. It seems that we somehow skipped the jet lag and got right on LA time. Benefit of being two world-class travelers, I suppose."

"I think it's because we feel so cozy together."

"That we do," he agreed, brushing the hair from her face. "What do you feel like doing? Do you want to get a workout in? Or are you hungry?"

"Yes to both, but first show me everything," she replied, breaking into a wide smile. "I'm ready to see where we live. Come on," she said, dragging him out of bed. "I'm too excited to wait."

They quickly got dressed in their gym clothes and then wandered through the house hand in hand. Ella's eyes widened as they entered each new room. "And obviously, this is the kitchen," Finn said.

"Wow! It's a chef's dream," she cooed, running her hand along the white marble island. "Oh, and you have eight burners. How wonderful for entertaining friends. Look at all this produce," she remarked, admiring the bowls overflowing with fresh fruits. "Avocados are my absolute favorite."

"We have avocado and lemon trees out back. Plus, Joyce goes to the farmers market a couple of times a week to pick up fresh, seasonal food."

"I'd love to go with her sometime."

"I'm sure she'd enjoy the company. There's just one room left on our tour. I've been saving it for last."

Finn took her hand and led her upstairs. As they approached the closed double doors, he said, "This is the room I had in mind for your office. It's empty now, but my decorator is coming by tomorrow afternoon so you two can plan and scheme. When you see it, just remember: we'll redo it from top to bottom, flooring to light fixtures."

"Oh my God," she gasped as he opened the doors to a massive room featuring sky-high ceilings and windows to match. "It's big enough to be a ballroom!"

He smiled. "You spend your life writing about the big topics, the big questions, and I hoped this big space might be inspiring." She silently let her eyes follow the crown molding around the entire ceiling as she tried to catch her breath. He took her hand and continued showing her around. "There's a full bathroom over here, and in this corner there's a walk-in closet. We could install some built-in cabinets and shelves. But just wait—I think you'll really love this bit," he said, leading her to a pair of doors. They stepped outside onto a large, furnished veranda with an outdoor fireplace, overlooking the entire back of the property. He rubbed her fingers and asked, "Do you think this will work for your office, sweetheart?"

"Do I think this will work?" she whispered incredulously, her voice shaking. She turned to him with tears in her eyes. "Finn, this is the nicest room in the house."

"I think so too," he said.

"No, I mean . . ."

"What, baby?"

"It's just lovely beyond words that you would save this for me."

He kissed her softly. "I've been picturing you here for so long, waiting to see how you would make this space your own."

"I can't even imagine what I'll write here."

"Something brilliant that pushes the bounds, no doubt. And I'll be the first in line to read it." She gazed into his eyes and pressed her forehead to his. After a quiet, intimate moment, he pulled back and asked, "Should we grab a quick workout and then something to eat?"

AN HOUR LATER, FRESHLY SHOWERED and dressed, they meandered into the kitchen.

"I'm starving," Finn said.

"Good. I'm going to make us a special brunch," Ella replied. "What do you feel like eating?"

"Anything. I'm easy. How can I help?"

"Maybe you could make your coffee and my tea. I'll take care of everything else."

"Okay, baby," he replied, grazing her hand as he passed.

"Wow, you've got everything in here," Ella remarked, peering inside the enormous stainless-steel refrigerator. "Ooh, there's crabmeat. Do you think your cook is saving that for something in particular?"

"No, baby. Everything in the house is for us. You can use anything you like."

"This will be fun," she said, piling food in her arms. "After you make the drinks, go relax in the dining room. I want to surprise you."

"Can I help you find anything?"

"I'm going to have to figure out where things are anyway. No time to learn like the present. Don't worry, I'll be fine," she assured him, opening and shutting several cabinets before retrieving a glass bowl.

Finn was relaxing in the dining room as instructed when Ella appeared with two mouthwatering plates, the food impeccably arranged like art.

"Wow!" Finn exclaimed. "This looks and smells amazing."

"Crab crepes with a mushroom cream sauce and a kale and avocado salad. I usually try to eat a little cleaner than this, but today is special. Think of it as Paris comes to LA," she explained, taking her seat.

"Thank you. It looks phenomenal."

"My pleasure."

Ella took a bite while Finn just sat, positively beaming at her.

She finished chewing and asked, "Aren't you going to try it?"

"I'm sorry, I got distracted. I'm just elated that you're here. I've imagined what this would be like every day since . . . Anyway, it's a dream come true." She rubbed his hand, and then he picked up his utensils and took a big bite of the crepe. "Wow, that's incredible."

"Glad you like it."

"After we eat, what do you say to spending the day lounging in the sunshine, swimming, and making love over and over again?"

She smiled. "I'm all in."

"OUR SECOND MORNING WAKING UP together in our home, with you in my arms. There are no words to describe how good this feels, how right it feels," Finn said.

"I wish we could stay like this all day. Or better yet, forever."

"Me too. But it's an exciting day—lots to do. First, you'll meet the house staff. Later, my assistant is coming by to go over some things. Then this afternoon, you'll meet with the decorator to get started on your office."

She glanced down and seemed to withdraw. He touched her chin, pulling her eyes back up to him.

"What is it, love? Are you still uncomfortable about my staff?"

"Well, you know I always love meeting new people. It's just . . . I've never had people milling around the place I live, except for this one commune where I stayed for a couple of months. But that was eons ago."

He laughed.

"It's just different having a household staff, that's all."

"They're just here to make things easier so we can focus on our work, traveling, whatever is important to us, and maybe someday, a family. They won't be in your way, and if there's anything they do that you want changed, that's no problem."

"How many of them are there?" she asked.

Finn chuckled. "You make them sound like an invading army."

"Well . . ."

"There's Joyce, our chef. She's also the head of the household staff. She's as nice as can be, and I just know you two will hit it off right away. There's nothing intimidating about her, so you can get that worried look off your face."

She giggled.

"Joyce brings in a sous-chef sometimes, especially if we want to throw a party or something. Then there are two cleaners and two groundskeepers; they take care of the garden, the pool, and whatever small stuff needs fixing around here. Finally, there's my personal assistant, Jason. He runs errands, makes reservations—that sort of thing. He'll be at your beck and call for anything you need, or he can make himself scarce if what you need is privacy."

"There's nothing I need that I can't do for myself."

"I have no doubt about that," he replied with a smile. "But he's here to be helpful."

"That's everyone, right?" she asked.

He laughed. "Yeah, baby, that's it. You'll feel better when you meet them. Speaking of which, what shall they call you?"

"What do you mean?"

"They call me Mr. Forrester. They could call you Ms. Sinclair. If you're planning to change your name when we get married, they could call you Mrs. Forrester."

"Finn . . ." she mumbled, squirming a bit and looking down.

"There's no pressure. I don't expect you to change your name. It's totally up to you."

"It's not that. It's just that I'm not very formal. I can't imagine people I see every day calling me by my last name. That's no way to be friendly or make things homey."

He smiled. "Would you prefer to be called Ella?"

She nodded.

"Okay, sweetheart. From now on, we're Finn and Ella to everyone. Should we make ourselves look a bit more presentable?"

"Yes, but Finn, just one more thing. I am planning to take your name; I thought I'd go by Ella Sinclair Forrester after we get married. If we're lucky enough to have children, they would have both our names too."

He smiled widely, lifted her hand to his lips, and kissed it.

"**ELLA WILL BE DOWN ANY MINUTE,** but I wanted to speak with you all first," Finn said to his staff, who were huddled around him in the kitchen. "Ella isn't comfortable with formality, so from now on, please address us both by our first names."

"Certainly, Mr. Forrester. Oh, I mean, Finn," Joyce replied, adjusting her thick-rimmed glasses.

He smiled. "I know it may take some getting used to, but there are going to be a few changes around here. Ella may have different preferences or ways of doing things, and I want to be sure we prioritize her wishes. She enjoys cooking and wants to be involved with the shopping. In fact, she recently wrote a book about food and pleasure. You two should have plenty in common, Joyce."

"We're all very much looking forward to meeting her. I've been with you the longest, so on behalf of all of us, we couldn't be happier for you," Joyce said.

"Thank you," Finn said with a genuine smile. "There is nothing more important to me than Ella's happiness. Nothing. I'm counting on all of you to do everything you can to make her feel at home."

They all nodded in acknowledgment just as Ella ambled into the room wearing a long, flowing gray sundress. "I'm sorry if I'm interrupting," she said, fidgeting with her beaded necklace.

"Don't be silly, sweetheart," Finn replied, placing his hand on the small of her back. "Everyone's eager to meet you." He made the introductions, and everyone said hello to one another.

"We're all so happy to welcome you," Joyce said, her warm smile much larger than her five-foot frame.

"Thank you," Ella replied.

"I thought maybe we could sit down and have a good chat, get to know each other a little. You can tell me the kinds of things you like to eat so we can plan some menus, what sort of food you'd like to have in the house, when you prefer to have meals, that sort of thing. I know you're interested in doing some of the cooking yourself, so you can tell me more about that and how I can be of assistance."

"That would be great. Thank you, Joyce," Ella replied.

"Yes, thank you," Finn added.

Joyce smiled. "There's coffee, tea, and freshly squeezed juice in the dining room. I'll bring your breakfast in soon, and then whenever you have time, we can have that chat, Ella. I'm looking forward to it."

Finn took Ella's hand and they strolled to the dining room. "See, that wasn't so bad, was it?" he asked as he pulled out her chair.

"Well, they didn't look like serial killers, so the food probably isn't poisoned."

He laughed and kissed the top of her head.

"THERE YOU ARE," ELLA SAID AS SHE strolled into the den and plopped down on the sofa beside Finn. "You were right. Joyce is wonderful. We had such fun getting to know each other. I can tell that we'll be fast friends."

"I told you," he said.

"I heard the doorbell and a bit of a commotion. More invaders?" she asked.

He chuckled. "Jason, my assistant, is here, and your things arrived from Paris. He's directing the movers—they're putting the boxes labeled 'books' and 'work' outside your office, the ones marked 'clothes' in our closet, and your keepsake chest in our bedroom. I figured you wouldn't want him to unpack for you, but of course he'd be happy to do it."

"I can unpack myself," she said.

Just then, Jason bounded into the room with a backpack slung over his shoulder. "You must be Ella. It's great to finally meet you!" he said, extending his hand.

"Likewise," she replied, standing to greet him. "Thank you for the clothes and personal items you got for me. They sure made it easy to settle in."

"I'm so glad. I can't take credit, though; Finn was very specific about what to get. Please, sit and get comfy. We have some things to go over."

They took a seat and Finn draped his arm around Ella.

"First things first," he said, unzipping his knapsack. "Here's my card with my phone number. Call or text anytime, day or night. Here is your set of keys to the house. We can go over the alarm system later. I figured you'd want to select your own code."

"Okay, great."

"Here's a credit card. There's no limit. It's already activated, so all you have to do is sign the back," he explained, handing her a credit card with her name on it.

She turned to Finn with a bewildered expression. "What on earth is this for?"

"So you can buy whatever you need," Finn replied. "You know, if you want clothes or . . ."

"Finn, there's nothing I need," she said quietly.

"You may want to get things for the house, maybe for your office. You can use it for absolutely anything. Never hesitate."

"Finn . . ."

"If I may interject," Jason said. Ella looked at him, a bit startled, and he continued, "If you'd prefer to have me pick things up for you, that's fine. In fact, I was planning on it. I brought a stack of designer catalogs so you can flip through them at your leisure and circle the styles you like," he said, placing the booklets on the coffee table. "That way, when I do personal shopping for you, I'll have some guidelines for your taste until we get to know each other better. Don't worry, I'm a whiz at picking accessories to complement any look."

"Uh, well, thank you," Ella stuttered. "It's just . . . well, it's just that I don't need anything. Really. I'm fine with what I have. Clothes aren't important to me."

Jason smiled. "That's absolutely fine. Based on the sundresses Finn had me get, I can tell you have a fabulous, casual, boho vibe. As you settle in, we can always add to your wardrobe. With all the buzz that *Celebration* is receiving, it looks like Finn will have a busy awards season ahead of him. When the time comes, I can help you select gowns."

"Oh, well, okay," Ella murmured, furrowing her brow as she tried to process everything.

Finn rubbed her arm.

Picking up on her uneasiness, Jason looked at her sympathetically. "I'm sure it feels like a lot. Moving to a new place, meeting new people, having all of this thrown at you. Please, rest assured, my only job is to make things easier for you."

"That's kind of you," she replied, still visibly tense.

"Look, I don't want to come off like a fanboy, but I know who you are. I mean, besides being Finn's fiancée. I've been reading your mind-shattering books and essays for years." Ella blushed. "I love working with Finn, and it will be an honor to get to know you too. There's no mold you have to fit. I'm here to learn what works for you. Just think of me as someone available to free up your time for work or the things that inspire you."

She smiled and a glimmer of relief crossed her face. "I appreciate that, really I do."

"Here," he said, whipping out another card and handing it to her. "I assumed you'd want a library card for research."

"That was thoughtful. Helpful too," she said, her smile growing.

"Just one last thing because I get the sense you've had enough thrown at you today." She giggled, and he placed a stack of car brochures on the table in front of her. "If you could tell me what kind of car you might be interested in, I can have some brought over for test-drives. Those are the latest by Porsche, Mercedes, Aston Martin, Jaguar, and so on."

Ella stammered, trying and failing to find the right words.

"If you're not sure which you'd like best, you can just tell me whether you'd prefer an SUV, a sedan, or something sporty. Even just the color you like would help. I'm guessing black, but maybe silver?"

She turned to Finn, and he gave her waist a gentle squeeze. "What is it, baby?"

She turned back to Jason and asked, "Can I have time to think about all of this?"

"Sure thing. That's exactly why I brought the brochures. Take all the time you want, and then you can reach out when you're ready. Or Finn can get in touch with me."

"Okay, thank you." She stood up and said, "If you two don't mind, I'd like to go unpack my things."

"Of course. I'll be up in a bit," Finn said, touching her hand.

"Ella, it was a real pleasure to meet you. Please let me know how I can be of assistance," Jason said.

She nodded. "Nice to meet you too."

A LITTLE WHILE LATER, FINN FOUND Ella sitting on the floor of their closet, folding her clothes.

"How's it going?" he asked.

"Fine. I don't have very much, so it's easy. I guess if you had your way, the closet would be overflowing."

"Ella," he said softly, sitting down beside her.

"When we fell in love, we spent months together in that charming room at the inn. I felt like we had everything we would ever need, just being cozy and close. You said you felt it too, that we could even live in my little loft in Paris. I always pictured us that way. In my fondest dream, I imagined us in a little cottage. Nothing fancy, just us. Someday we'd fill it with our family, tripping all over each other." She sighed and added, "It doesn't seem like you could ever be happy that way."

"That isn't true."

She looked him straight in his eyes and said, "Finn, why are you doing this? I don't understand."

"Doing what?" he asked, stroking her cheek.

"Trying to Cinderella me."

"That's not how I meant any of this."

"Don't you know how much I love you?" she asked. "I only want you. I don't care about anything else."

"Sweetheart, I'm not trying to change you, or buy you, or control you. All I want in this world is to make you happy and for us to be together."

"But we are together, and I am happy. I don't need anything else. Why don't you believe me?"

"You uprooted your life for me, and I . . ."

"What?"

"I don't take that responsibility lightly," Finn said.

"I want to be here with you. You don't need to buy me anything."

"Sweetheart, I'm just trying to make your life easier. I mean, how are you going to get around in LA? You'll need a car. The alternative would be a car and driver, but I figured you'd hate that. You're too independent, and I know you'll want to be able to come and go as you please to see friends or whatever."

"I guess that's true." She paused in thought. "But I don't want something so fancy. Just a simple, safe car to get me around."

"Okay, baby. As for the clothes and stuff, that's only if you decide that you want something. As far as I'm concerned, you could wear this sundress every day for the rest of your life. You are so beautiful." She blushed. "I just thought you might want some things for the LA climate, or for when we travel, or for the Hollywood stuff I have to do from time to time. That's all. If there's something you want for the house, I didn't want you to have to fret over it or feel like you had to ask me."

"That's sweet. It is. You are the most generous man. I'm sorry I took it the wrong way."

"You have nothing to apologize for."

"Finn, we're building a life together, and . . ." He waited patiently for her to find the words. "And I want to make sure that we love each other as we are. As we truly are. Always."

"I do, Ella. I know you and love you with all my heart."

THAT AFTERNOON, ELLA WAS LYING in bed reading a book when Finn came into the room. "Sweetheart, the decorator is here. We set up a folding table and chairs in your office, and Joyce made you two a pot of tea."

She smiled and followed him to the room.

"Ella, this is Lorraine," he said.

"Pleased to meet you," Ella said. "The furniture you picked out for the bedroom is gorgeous."

Lorraine smiled widely, revealing dimpled cheeks. "I'm so glad you like it. I'm excited to transform this room into something very special. We're going to have some fun."

"I'll leave you two to it," Finn said, giving Ella a delicate kiss before exiting.

Lorraine jubilantly squeezed Ella's wrists, positive energy oozing out of her. "This space is fabulous. Best room in the house, if you ask me."

"Yeah, it's amazing. I don't know how I could possibly fill it."

"Well, that's what we're here to figure out. Shall we sit and get to know each other?" They plopped down at the table and Lorraine said, "Why don't you tell me about how you plan to use this room, the functions it should serve, and the vibe you're after. I know you're a writer, so I imagine you'll need a desk and some little touches for inspiration."

Ella smiled, and her shoulders relaxed as she began to feel at ease. "Yes, I'll need a desk and maybe some bookshelves. I like to socialize and collaborate with other artists and intellectuals, so maybe a sitting area with a couch and a couple of chairs would be nice."

"Excellent. I already have all kinds of ideas about how we might arrange things for the best flow. I brought several binders with me," Lorraine noted, gesturing at the materials strewn on the table. "They cover everything: flooring, color palettes, furniture styles, themes. You can tell me some more about your work, and then we can start flipping through them to see what style suits you best."

NEARLY TWO HOURS LATER, FINN lightly tapped on the door before coming in. The women were laughing uproariously. "I didn't want to interrupt, but I just wanted to see if you two could use more tea."

"You're not interrupting at all," Ella replied. "We've been having a ball."

"Yes, Ella is a hoot. I think I have everything I need to get started," Lorraine said, scooping up her folders. "This room is going to be my masterpiece, my magnum opus."

Ella giggled. "If you don't mind, I want to go check on my kitten. Please excuse me. It was lovely to meet you, Lorraine."

"She's in our room," Finn said.

After Ella left, Lorraine said, "She's absolutely delightful. Her spirit is infectious. I can see why you're so smitten."

Finn blushed. "Now you know why it's so important to me that this room comes out just right."

"Don't worry, it's going to be magnificent. I estimate that it will take at least a few weeks to do it right, even working at full speed. My contractor is standing by with a team. The style is going to be French country, white with green pops, plenty of antiques with a few modern touches. I'm going to start scouring my sources in Europe for the perfect antique writing desk. Ella has great, eclectic taste. She didn't ask for much, but she gave me lots to work with in terms of her lifestyle and aesthetic."

"Please do absolutely everything she asked for. There are a few ideas I have too, a few surprises. This room has to be more than an office. I want it to show Ella exactly how I feel."

 **CHAPTER 4**

"That was mind-blowing," Finn said, rolling onto the bed beside Ella. "You are so sexy."

"I'm going to miss you tomorrow. I've had so much fun with you these past couple of weeks, lounging about, exploring the hiking trails, talking for hours."

"It will be hard to tear myself away, especially to do press junkets. They can be so boring, and I'd much rather be here with you. But with Willow busy in New York rehearsing for her play and Charlotte in London, Michael and I are doing the lion's share of promotion. I'm eager to catch up with him and find out how on earth he got Lauren back."

Ella giggled. "Just make sure he's being a good boy so he doesn't foul it up again. Losing someone you love once is heartbreaking; to lose them twice would be unimaginable."

"It sure would," he agreed, tracing his finger along her hairline. They stared at each other for a long moment, the energy between them electric. Finally, Finn said, "What about you? I saw that you set up your laptop and notebooks on the dining room table. Planning to get started on your next project?"

"Yes! Until my office is ready, I thought I'd just plop down there, if that's okay."

"Of course it is."

"I promised Lorraine that I wouldn't peek at the room until it's done, so I don't even know what they're doing in there. She warned me there would be construction this week and it might get noisy. So, I'm meeting an old friend from college at a vegan café and bookshop in Venice Beach."

"Not an old flame, I hope," he said playfully as he tucked a strand of hair behind her ear. "Should I be jealous?"

"Never. We belong to each other, you and I," she replied, giving him a smooch. "My friend Marni lives in LA, and I've been looking forward to seeing her after all these years. We were tight in college, founding members of our school's philosophy club. Now she's the editor at an arts and culture magazine that publishes a lot of highbrow theoretical essays. She's feminist, snarky, and smart. I emailed her when I moved here, and we've been chatting ever since." He smiled and she continued, "The best part is, she told me she runs a small philosophy group, just her and a couple of other people: a philosophy professor and some sort of conceptual artist. Apparently, they meet once a week for tea or whatever and to talk about big ideas or things they've read. They're both coming tomorrow too, and she said I can join their group if I'm interested. I've always had lots of friends who are thinkers and creatives. It fuels my work, and I was worried about whether I'd have that here. This could be the solution."

"That's great, sweetheart," he said, unable to tame his smile.

"What's that grin about?" she asked.

"I just want you to be happy and fulfilled, that's all. And . . ."

"What?"

"I'm happy to see you building a life here."

"Well, that's the whole point, silly." She turned onto her side and whispered, "Sweet dreams. Now switch off the light and spoon me, my love."

"JUST A LITTLE FINISHING SPRAY AND you'll be all set," the young makeup artist said.

"Good job. You really know your stuff," Michael replied.

She giggled, batting her false eyelashes. "Well, it's easy with you." She cleared her throat and said, "Someone will come get you two as soon as the reporter is ready."

Michael turned to gawk as she exited the room.

Finn laughed. "Some things never change. The first time you and I met was in the makeup trailer in Sweden. As I recall, you ended up sleeping with the makeup artist, not to mention half a dozen extras."

"Those days are behind me, but it doesn't hurt to look," he said with a smarmy smile.

"I wonder if Lauren would feel that way."

Michael shrugged unconcernedly.

"You two looked solid in Cannes. When I saw you with your daughter the day after the premier, you seemed like a family."

"We are. It's been great."

"How the hell did you get her to take you back, anyway?" Finn asked with a chuckle.

"It wasn't easy. The night I got home from filming, I called her. Convinced her to go out to dinner with me and Sophie. We went to some tacky little place they both like, a far cry from what I'm used to. Before long, we were laughing hysterically, and the cheap decor and kid-friendly food didn't seem so bad. We could have shut that place down. Being with them felt great, like coming home. I was ready to slip right into family life."

"Wow. I'm speechless."

"Yeah, it shocked the hell out of me too. Unfortunately, Lauren was much more hesitant. I pursued her relentlessly, trying to prove myself. I wanted to show her that I'm a changed man. I showered her with flowers, chocolates, balloons, and I even sent her a singing telegram, but she was having none of it. She made me promise not to have sex with anyone else while we spent time together and got to know each other again. She said something about rebuilding trust."

"And? Did you abstain?"

Michael huffed. "Yeah, but let me tell you, it was pure torture."

Finn laughed.

"Eventually, she opened herself back up to me. The thing is, we were always in love. I guess that connection doesn't go away. Plus, we have a kid together. So, after months of that 'proving myself' bullshit, we decided to do it for real this time. I bought us a little house, and we've been living together as a family."

"Wow, that's great."

"Yeah, well, I still kept my old apartment. You know, just in case."

Finn chuckled. "I say this to you in the spirit of friendship: don't fuck it up. Remember how much you missed her and regretted things. No matter how many women you were with, it was clear that no one could take her place. Try to get it right this time. You're lucky you got a second chance—don't blow it."

"Speaking of second chances, how's it going with Ella? You two certainly caused quite a commotion at Cannes. Are you living happily ever after?"

"Michael, it's bliss. She moved in with me right after Cannes. I can't even describe how good it feels to be with her again, forever this time. Nothing has ever felt better."

"I'm impressed."

"How so?"

"Well, just that you were able to get over her leaving you like that," Michael said. "She broke your heart. It was brutal. Plus . . ."

"What?"

"Ella's such a free spirit, so bohemian. I'm impressed you got her to settle down. Good for you. I'm happy for you."

"Yeah, thanks," Finn mumbled, looking down.

Just then, an assistant came into the room. "They're ready for you both."   ·

"THIS PLACE IS REALLY CUTE. Super earthy-crunchy," Ella observed.

"Yeah," Marni replied, pulling her dark shoulder-length hair into a scrunchie. "Dante's vegan, so he knows all the best spots where the food tastes like real food and not children's paste. It's very Cali."

Ella laughed. "When in LA."

"We usually try to meet at one of our places, but Jade's having roommate trouble, Dante's apartment is a mess with some big art project he's working on, and my bungalow is a bit too far for everyone to schlep," Marni explained. "You'll love them. Dante's a gifted experimental artist. He studied philosophy and fine art, and he makes the most provocative installations about the embodied Black experience, referencing everyone from Bordo to Baldwin. Jade teaches philosophy at USC. She's kind of all work and no play, but she's super smart. As fate would have it, she's used your writing in her contemporary philosophy class. I guess she's a fan!"

"I'm excited to have people to talk to about work again. I had a great group of friends in Paris—artists, writers . . ."

"Well, I, for one, am thrilled you're in LA."

Ella smiled. "So, catch me up. Are you seeing anyone?"

"Who has the time? I was dating a woman kind of seriously for a while, but it didn't work out. She wanted too much. You know me: work is my life. My version of 'having it all' is doing big things in the world and then going home to a bottle of pinot noir and a remote control I don't have to share with anyone." Ella laughed and Marni continued, "But I hear you've gone all glass slipper on me. I'm telling you, Ella, my eyes nearly popped out of my head when I saw Finn Forrester propose to you at Cannes. I was watching TV and mindlessly munching on some popcorn when I saw the news. I literally choked on a kernel. Could have died in my apartment!"

Ella laughed. "What can I say? He swept me off my feet."

"Does he respect your work? I mean, you're not going to morph into one of those *Real Housewives of Hollywood* zombie plastic things, right? You're a feminist icon. You can't fuck us over and jump ship now."

"Don't worry, no plans to zombie out. Finn and I are both passionate about our own work, just like we are about each other."

"Good, then let's skip ahead to the sex talk. Seriously, Ella, he's crazy hot. Ah, and speaking of hot, there's Dante," Marni said, lowering her voice. "Fair warning, he may be the most gorgeous Black man on the planet. I say that as a committed lesbian."

Ella tried to muffle her laughter as Dante approached the table. Marni jumped up and hugged him. They both sat down, and she said, "Dante, this is my good friend—"

"Gabriella Sinclair. I would know you anywhere. If you weren't taken, I'd already be wooing you. Beautiful and brilliant. Your essay on eroticism inspired one of my recent pieces."

"I'm flattered. Please, call me Ella."

"So, before Jade gets here and makes us talk about Sartre's *Nausea* until our ears bleed, I want the scoop. How did one of the most brilliant philosophers of our time end up in La-La Land and engaged to a Hollywood legend? Spill."

"HONEY, I'M HOME," FINN CALLED as he joined Ella in the dining room and gave her a peck. "Sorry, I've always wanted to say that."

"Perfect timing. I just poured us each a bourbon. How did your press thing go?" she asked as they sat down.

"Fine. Same old drill: trying to be enthusiastic while answering the same questions all day. Of course, the first thing every reporter asked about was you—how we met, when we're getting married. Michael was a good wingman, though. He made jokes and eventually steered them back to talking about the film."

"See? His bravado comes in handy from time to time."

Finn laughed and asked, "How was your day? Did you have a good time catching up with your friend?"

"It was great. We were super close in school but lost touch since I was always roaming around. I forgot how much I like hanging out with her. Her friends are great too. Really smart and interesting, and they're familiar with my work. I'm officially a member of their philosophy club now."

"That's great, sweetheart."

"We meet once a week and take turns hosting. I thought it might be nice to invite them here next week. Would that be okay?"

"Sweetheart, this is your home. You can have guests here any time you like. You don't need to ask anyone's permission."

Ella smiled. "I know you have that voice-over job next week, but if you're able to stop by to meet them . . ."

"I'll make a point of it."

"Would you mind if I gave Marni a call before dinner?"

"Of course not."

"I'll be quick," she said, slipping her cell phone out of her pocket to make the call. "Hey, Marni, it's Ella. I just wanted to let you know that it's no problem, we can have next week's meeting at Finn's house."

Finn winced but tried to muster a smile as Ella wrapped up her call.

Just then, Joyce came into the room to serve their dinner. "Ooh, this looks delicious," Ella remarked, admiring the pan-seared scallops atop a bed of roasted vegetables. "Joyce, I'm having a few friends over next week. I'd like to serve cake with coffee and tea in the living room. I have a few recipes in mind, but I thought maybe you could help me."

"My pleasure. Find me whenever you're free and we can go over the shopping list."

Ella turned to Finn. "This looks so good. I'm starving."

He feigned a smile and picked up his fork.

"'FINN'S HOUSE.' THOSE WERE HER exact words," Finn said to Michael. "That's how she thinks of it, as my house, not hers."

"Relax, she's only lived there a couple of weeks. She's just getting used to things."

"I hope so, but you said yourself that Ella's never been one to settle down. Maybe . . ."

"Didn't you say she's mentioned having kids some-day?" Michael asked. "She must be in this thing for real if she's making plans for a family."

"Yeah, but we talked about that in Sweden too, and she still . . ."

"Listen, I saw her on the red carpet in Cannes before you arrived. She was a nervous wreck, waiting to see you. The next day, when we all hung out, she said she'd never been happier, that she couldn't wait to marry you. She's completely head over heels for you."

Finn exhaled. "You're right. I trust what we have. I just want to do everything right this time. I have to make things perfect for her."

"I'm telling you, relax. She just needs to adjust."

"Yeah."

"But if you're really worried that this thing could blow up at any minute and you'll look ridiculous after that whirlwind of an engagement, I'll get the press to back off on the questions about Ella."

Finn sighed and his shoulders slumped.

 **CHAPTER 5**

"Yes, but even Aristotle recognized that art cannot be a slave to reality," Dante said.

"That cycles us back to the nature of representations," Jade mused. "Ella, what do you think?"

"I think I need some more fuel. Who wants a refill?" she asked.

"Ooh, I'd love some more green tea," Jade said.

"I'll take more oolong," Marni added.

Ella refilled each cup. "Would anyone like another slice of cake?"

"Uh, I will. The cherry, please," Marni replied, holding out her plate. "I still can't believe you made these from scratch."

"I've always loved baking," Ella said as she served her a piece of cake with a dollop of homemade vegan whipped topping.

"I wonder if the world would be surprised to learn that the woman who reimagined women's sexuality spends her time at home baking," Marni said.

"As far as I'm concerned, baking is all about the pleasure principle," Ella quipped. "Besides, it can be erotic. You should see me lick the bowl."

Everyone erupted into laughter.

"And you'd be amazed by what I can do with a rolling pin," Ella added. They were laughing so hard they were clutching their stomachs when Finn walked into the room.

"Well, this sounds like fun. I hope I'm not interrupting," he said.

"Not possible," she replied, rising to give him a kiss. "Finn, these are my friends, Marni, Dante, and Jade."

"Nice to meet you all," he said.

They all nodded and smiled. "Thanks for letting our little club crash your house," Marni said.

"Any time. Ella and I are always happy to have guests in our home."

"Why don't you join us, my love?" Ella suggested. "I made a sour cherry–vanilla cake and a flourless chocolate torte. Indulge with us."

"I wish I could, sweetheart; they look incredible. It was all I could do to run out for a minute. Sadly, I'm needed back at the studio. Looks like we might be able to wrap this thing up today. I just wanted to stop by to meet your friends."

"That was sweet of you," she said.

Finn gave her waist a gentle squeeze and lightly pressed his mouth to hers. "I'll see you tonight, sweetheart. Save me a piece of that chocolate cake." He turned to the group and said, "Great to meet you all. Hope to see you again soon."

After he left, Ella asked, "So, where were we? Baking: home economics or sex ed?"

THAT NIGHT, ELLA WAS SNUG IN BED reading a philosophy tome while Finn reviewed a script his agent had sent. Bored with her book, she placed it on her lap and sat quietly, absentmindedly running her fingers down his arm.

"That feels nice," he said, tossing his script onto the nightstand to give her his full attention.

"You are the sweetest man. Thank you for stopping by today to meet everyone."

"It was my pleasure. I'm only sorry I couldn't stay longer."

"They all thought it was sweet too. And they loved your house."

He stroked the side of her face and gently said, "Ella, this is *our* house."

"You know what I mean," she said dismissively.

"But Ella . . ."

"Dante is an amazing artist. I scrolled through his website. You'd appreciate his work; it has a great storytelling quality. He really pushes people to think. We're meeting at his place next week, so I'll get to see his works in progress."

"That's great, but please tell me he's gay."

"Why? You got a crush?" she joked.

"It was hard not to notice that he's an incredibly good-looking guy. Maybe I'm just a little jealous."

Ella giggled. "Sorry to disappoint, but he's definitely not gay. Marni is, if you're looking to add more gay friends to your inner circle."

He laughed. "Good one. Seriously, though, I'm glad you've found some creative people to spend time with. I know how important that is to you."

"Finn . . ." She trailed off, looking down.

"What is it, baby?"

"Well, it's just that your parents don't live far from here, and I know you're close with them. And you told me how much you like to hang out with your friends, but you haven't seen any of them the whole time we've been here."

"That's because I've been working and spending all my free time with you."

"I know, but . . ."

"What?" Finn asked.

"You haven't introduced me to anyone in your life, only the people on your payroll. Do your friends and family all hate me? Is that the problem?"

"God, no! Nothing of the sort. Why would you think such a thing?"

"Because of our breakup. You must have told your friends and family about it. Do they all think I'm a bitch? Is that why you haven't introduced me to them yet?"

"Oh, baby, no," he insisted, caressing her cheek. "When I got home from Sweden, I told everyone about you, my parents, my friends, everyone. I told them that I had met the love of my life, the woman I was going to marry. I said you had some things that you needed to take care of in your own life, but when you were ready, we'd be together."

"Really? That's what you said?" she asked, her eyes becoming misty.

"Word for word. Sweetheart, everyone in my life has been texting me nonstop since our very public engagement, begging for the chance to meet you. The only reason I haven't mentioned it is because I didn't want to overwhelm or pressure you. I know it's been a lot, moving here, getting settled. I just didn't want to ask for too much too soon."

"You really are the sweetest man. Finn, I want to build our life together. I would love to meet anyone and everyone who's important to you."

"I'll call them all first thing in the morning. I'm sure my parents will jump at the chance to meet you. Then maybe we could invite my closest friends over for a barbecue. There are two married couples, Chuck and Carol and Tom and Elise, and a couple of single guys, Dan and Jim, buddies of mine since we were kids. How about a week from Saturday? Joyce can handle the arrangements."

"That sounds perfect, but please let me take care of everything."

"Okay, sweetheart. They'll be thrilled to meet you."

Ella smiled. "What do you think about inviting Michael and Lauren too? It would be nice to get to know her better."

"I'm on it."

THE NEXT MORNING, ELLA WOKE UP and stretched her arms. She rolled over and discovered Finn wasn't there, but there was a note on her nightstand: *Went to run a quick errand. Love, Finn.*

She slipped her robe on and brushed her teeth. When she emerged from the bathroom, Finn was waiting for her holding a vase overflowing with brightly colored wildflowers.

Her whole face lit up. "Oh, wow. Those are stunning."

"God, you're beautiful in the morning," he said as he placed the vase on her vanity.

Ella blushed and asked, "What's the occasion?"

"I was thinking about that incredible night in Sweden when we had that special dinner in your room and . . ."

"You had it sent up with a small vase of wildflowers."

He nodded. "Then we took a candlelit bubble bath in that huge clawfoot tub, and we talked about building a life together, making an adventure, having a family."

"I remember every word."

"Now we're living that dream."

She gave him a soft kiss.

"I called my folks and they're stopping by later," Finn said. "They'll be here around two."

"What?" she asked, her eyes wide.

"They've been dying to meet you, so as soon as I mentioned it, they insisted on coming today."

"Oh my God, I need to get ready. There's so much to do. Should I serve a late lunch, or would they prefer . . ."

"You don't need to do anything. They're swinging by on their way to visit some friends. They can only stay for an hour or so. Joyce can serve tea and coffee."

"Then we'll need a cake. I know just the recipe. Oh, but I may need to run to the farmers market . . ." She trailed off, practically spinning in circles as she was speaking.

Finn gently took her hand. "You don't have to do anything. Just tell the staff what you want them to do."

"Finn, I'm meeting your parents for the very first time. This is important. I'm not outsourcing it. Although maybe Joyce can run to the farmers market so I'll have more time to . . ."

"Hey," he said, massaging her hand.

"Yeah?" she asked, looking deep into his eyes.

"I love you. That's all."

A FEW HOURS LATER, FINN FOUND Ella standing in their closet, her long hair wrapped in a towel.

"Hey, love. What are you up to?" he asked.

"Trying to decide what to wear," she replied, nervously pulling out hangers and shoving them back.

"I'm just wearing what I have on: jeans and a polo. Throw on anything."

"So you think I should wear jeans and not one of my usual sundresses?"

"Dress how you always do. You always look great. Just be yourself and relax."

"What about this one?" she asked, pulling out a long, flowing buttercup-yellow sundress.

"That would be perfect," he replied, pecking her cheek. "Baby, my parents are totally low-key. They're just excited to meet you."

"Are you sure they don't hate me?" she asked, distress marring her heart-shaped face.

He laughed. "Not in the slightest. They're eager to get to know you."

"You haven't told me much about them. I'm so nervous, I can't even remember their names."

"Daniel and Barbara. They're great, supportive, down-to-earth. In fact, you once paid me the nicest compliment." She raised her eyebrows and he said, "You said I was the kind of actor who considers the whole story he's a part of telling. That comes from my folks. When my mother started taking me to auditions, she'd tell me to 'be truthful' in my performances and to 'remember that people need their stories told.' They also never let me get caught up in the Hollywood nonsense. Early on, I started to become a bit enamored by fame, and they straightened me out right away. They told me to get over myself and that it's a privilege to be an artist, a privilege that requires humility. I wouldn't be who I am without them."

Ella smiled. "What do they do?"

"You'll have a lot in common with them. My mother worked part-time from home as a copy editor for academic authors. My dad was a civil rights law professor. But I retired them years ago."

"You did?"

"I bought them a house, nothing too showy, but something they're comfortable in. For years, I sent them on adventures around the world—Egypt, India, South Africa, Alaska. They've slowed down in that respect, but they still let me send them on a tropical cruise every year."

"That's lovely."

"Sweetheart, I'd love to do the same thing for your mother, if you'll let me. I'll take care of her. You won't have to worry about anything. I have the means to—"

"Finn, please, my mother is fine. You don't need to do anything for her."

He kissed her forehead. "I'm just saying I'll take care of you, and that includes anyone you love. Family is the most important thing to me."

"Tell me more about what Daniel and Barbara do these days," she said, trying to change the subject.

"They spend most of their time staying busy with activism and charity stuff. They're lefties, super progressive, so they're all over any cause related to fighting racism, supporting women's rights, feeding the hungry, or lobbying for environmental protections. They've campaigned for just about every liberal politician in the state of California, even down to the city council. Be warned: my mother is always signing me up for these protest email lists. You can't imagine the spam I get."

Ella laughed.

"Aside from that, they're avid readers and they love watching documentaries. It's hard to believe the wealth of information they know about different cultures, history, sociology, and the like. Think of them as hippie intellectuals."

"They sound great," she said.

"They are. And knowing them, they'll be right on time, so I should probably let you finish getting ready."

"Are you sure this dress is okay?" she asked again, her forehead creased with worry.

"It's perfect."

"MOM, DAD, IT'S GREAT TO SEE YOU," Finn said, hugging them each tightly. "Come on in." He took Ella's hand and proudly announced, "This is Ella. Ella, these are my parents, Daniel and Barbara."

"I'm so glad to finally meet you," Ella said.

"The feeling is mutual," Barbara replied, wrapping her in a big hug. "We've heard so many lovely things about you, and we've been dying to get to know you."

"Me too," Ella said.

"Congratulations on your engagement!" Barbara added.

"Yes, congratulations! We're just glad Finn finally let us come by to meet you. We weren't sure if he's been keeping you to himself or holding you hostage. If you need to make a break for it, just give us a signal," Daniel said with a wink.

Ella giggled and Finn said, "Let's go hang out in the living room. We set up snacks on the coffee table."

They ambled into the living room. Finn and Ella dropped onto the couch, where he slung his arm around her, and his parents sat in the surrounding chairs.

"This looks delicious," Barbara remarked, admiring the cake dusted with powdered sugar. "Looks like Joyce outdid herself."

"Actually, Ella made it," Finn said. "Here, let me serve everyone some tea and cake."

"It's just an old-fashioned butter cake with blueberries," Ella said.

"I'm sure my doctor would have a fit—she's always getting on me about my cholesterol—but it looks too good to pass up," Barbara said.

"This is scrumptious," Daniel raved, wiping powdered sugar off his lips after taking a hearty bite.

"Mmm, it's wonderful," Barbara agreed.

"Yeah, it's delicious, sweetheart," Finn said softly.

Ella smiled. "You can top it with any fruit, and it caramelizes as it bakes. I usually use apples or plums, but blueberries are special to us, so I thought for today . . ." she explained, rubbing Finn's thigh.

"Sweetheart, tell them the story about how Albie and Margaret met." Finn turned to his parents and said, "When I got back from that Jean Mercier film, I told you about how extraordinary it was working with Albie Hughes."

"Yes, you did, after you eventually stopped gushing about Ella," Daniel said.

Finn blushed. "Albie was one of a kind, as remarkable in life as he was on-screen. He told us the most wonderful story about how he met his wife, the love of his life, to whom he was married for forty years. Go on, tell them."

"It was at a party in London," Ella began. "Something completely uptight and pretentious, a total upper-crust soiree, which was definitely not Albie's style. Margaret ended up there by chance, with no idea what kind of party it was, so she showed up in a simple dress with a homemade blueberry pie. Albie was hit by lightning the moment he saw her standing there, so beautifully out of place. Eventually, he spotted her at the dessert table and sidled over to her. He took a piece of the pie she'd made, and they started talking. He said he fell madly in love with her on the spot." Finn rubbed her back and she continued, "Anyway, ever since we heard the story, blueberries make us think of love. Epic, crazy love." She crinkled her nose and shook her head. "Maybe it's silly, but they've become special to us." She looked at Finn, and he gently kissed her forehead. His parents watched with warm smiles across their faces.

"That's a lovely story," Barbara said. "It was so thoughtful of you to make this for us, but I hope we didn't put you to any trouble with our impromptu visit. We would have taken you kids out somewhere, but sometimes it's easier in private, because of . . ."

Ella looked at her quizzically.

"Well, sometimes it can be difficult for Finn in public. The attention, you know," Barbara explained.

"Oh! Yes, of course. I'm sorry, I always forget he's famous. Not that I don't realize he's an actor. Of course I do. We met on a film set, after all. And he's such a deeply talented artist," Ella stammered. "It's just that I think of him as Finn, that's all."

Barbara and Daniel smiled at one another and then at their son before Barbara said, "So, Ella, Finn tells us your mother is an artist and that she lives in Spain with her partner. How exciting. What kind of painting does she do?"

An hour later, they were laughing hysterically, all completely at ease. "I'm telling you," Daniel said, "these people have never read a book. Critical race theory isn't new. I was teaching it decades ago, before some of these pissants were alive. If I hear one more of them say that it's corrupting their babies, I'm going to lose my mind. Sadly, it isn't taught in preschool, so if their 'babies' are learning it, they're probably in graduate school. Pretty smart babies, especially considering how dumb their parents are."

Everyone cracked up.

"Ella, you must relate. I'm sure there's resistance to your work. Keep fighting it. Your insights into how culture corrupts the experience of pleasure is freeing women from the shackles of modern hegemony. It's recentering the discourse and pushing forward a new body politic grounded in women's experiences," Daniel noted.

"She's absolutely brilliant," Finn said, washed in a look of pride. He bashfully turned to Ella and quietly said, "It's true."

Barbara smiled, watching her son and his betrothed.

"Brilliant may be an overstatement, but I do like to push the bounds. If nothing else, it keeps this one on his toes," Ella replied, giving Finn's hand a squeeze.

"That it does," Finn agreed, looking down, his face turning red.

"Well, I know we could sit here and chat all day long," Barbara said. "It's just so wonderful spending time together, but I'm afraid if we don't leave soon, the traffic will be horrendous."

"We're so glad you could stop by," Finn said, rising to his feet.

"It was absolutely wonderful to meet you," Barbara said, hugging Ella. "Let's get together for lunch sometime. I know you're surely busy with work, but when you have time, I'd love to finish our conversation. Oh, and I'll add you to that email list I told you about so you can sign those petitions."

"Great," Ella replied, smiling as she shot a knowing glance at Finn.

"Sweetheart, I'm going to walk my folks out," Finn said, pecking her cheek.

When they got outside, Finn said, "Thanks so much for coming."

"Way to go, son! She's sensational," Daniel enthused. "Smart as a whip, kindhearted, and a real knockout to boot."

Finn smiled. "What do you think, Mom?"

"She's everything I ever hoped for you. She's her own person with her own interests and passions, someone who can be a real partner for you." She paused to consider her words, then said, "When you became so ridiculously successful at such a young age, I worried about the kind of woman you would end up with, if she would only see you as a movie star, and whether she would really love you for the remarkable man you are. Ella loves you, the real you, not the glossy image on the cover of GQ. It's clear as day that you're mad about her too. I couldn't get over the look on your face every time you glanced at her, like she's the only star in your universe. I've never seen you so happy."

"Being with her, it's everything I've ever wanted," Finn said.

"Your father and I are thrilled for you." He opened her car door and she got in. "Now don't forget to read that information I sent you about pollution in our oceans." With that, she shut her door and they drove away.

Finn returned inside and found Ella in the kitchen covering the leftover cake with plastic wrap. He came up behind her, slipped his arms around her waist, and whispered, "They loved you."

"I was a little nervous at first, but they made me feel so comfortable. They're great. I shouldn't be surprised. You're such an extraordinary man, it's no wonder you have such lovely parents. Seeing who they are helps me understand how you could be so grounded, value driven, and focused on love and family despite the whole Hollywood thing." She turned to face him and he kissed her. "It's nice they live close to us. If we have children someday, they'll be so lucky to have such wonderful grandparents nearby."

Finn smiled widely. He wove his fingers into her hair and kissed her again. "I love you."

A FEW DAYS LATER, THEY WERE CUDDLING on the couch and reading the morning newspaper when Lorraine popped over. "I have the final item for your office, Ella. I just need to hang it. Then it's time for the big reveal," she announced.

"Ooh, how exciting," Ella said.

"Sweetheart, I want to go up and take a look. Wait right here," Finn instructed.

"Okay," she replied.

He returned a few minutes later with a grin and said, "Come on, love." When they arrived at the door, he told her, "Close your eyes." She obliged. He took her hand and led her into the room. "Okay, open your eyes."

She opened her eyes and gasped. "Oh my God," she muttered, slowly twirling around to take it all in. "It's . . . it's the most beautiful room I've ever seen."

"We went with a three-tone wood parquet floor, ivory walls, and sheer matching curtains," Lorraine explained. "We've added this large window seat and built-in library over here, right when you walk in. Since you like to work with others, the center of the room is designed for collaboration with a plush white couch and comfortable chairs. I added pillows with a green ivy pattern and green throw blankets to give it a splash of color while staying true to the French country theme." Ella smiled softly, her eyes becoming damp. Lorraine continued, "The tea table is an antique imported from Scotland. It's a bit higher than your average coffee table, in case you want to sit there and write. Personally, the chandelier is my favorite piece in the room. It was handcrafted in the 1920s, and the strands feature over one thousand crystal balls. And you can see we've installed wooden beams on the ceiling, to mirror the style of your apartment in Paris."

Ella turned to Finn, who smiled brightly and whispered, "I remembered how you described your apartment."

"Over in the far corner, the pièce de résistance, is an antique writing desk, made in France, featuring two-tone wood and gold engravings on the legs," Lorraine said. "It belonged to Colette. Finn said she was one of your favorite writers."

"Oh my God," Ella mumbled, running her fingers across the desk. She turned to Finn and asked, "How . . . how . . ."

He rubbed her hand. "That night in Sweden when we played that game where everyone described who they would invite to a dinner party. You mentioned her."

"I . . . I don't know what to say."

"There's a lot to absorb," Lorraine said. "We've redone the bathroom, and over in the closet, we've installed shelves and drawers for better organization. It's already loaded up with your favorite notebooks and other supplies. I think Finn would like to show you the rest, so I'll see myself out."

"Thank you for everything, Lorraine," Finn said.

Ella turned and hugged her, whispering, "Thank you," in a barely audible voice.

"It was my great pleasure," Lorraine replied on her way out the door.

"Come here," Finn said, taking Ella's hand and directing her to the library. "The top shelf is poetry, all the Romantics. First editions. For when you want to get lost, or maybe found. Beneath that, philosophy books. Simone de Beauvoir and all your favorites." She sniffled and he continued, "The bathroom has a big clawfoot bathtub, like the one at the inn from that great night. Oh, come over here." Her eyes whirled as she took in all the details: a sparkling Eiffel Tower on a small table, an old map of Sweden, a stack of modern art books, a framed photo with the whole group from when they met on location, another photo of them kissing on the red carpet in Cannes, a pastel-colored globe sitting atop a gold base. He noticed her eyes land on the globe and explained, "To help us plan our adventures." She smiled, trying to hold back her tears. "That's the piece we were waiting for," Finn noted, pointing to a framed Jean-Michel Basquiat poster signed by the late artist. "He was another person you mentioned as a dream dinner guest. I thought it might serve as inspiration and a focal point for the sitting area when you have people over."

"Finn, I don't know what to say," she muttered, hot tears streaming down her face.

He gently wiped her tears. "There's still more to see. The outside is my favorite," he said, leading her to the newly installed French doors. "Go on."

Ella opened the doors and stepped onto the veranda. There was a hand-painted mural covering the entire wall that depicted landmarks from around the globe—the Arc de Triomphe, the Tokyo Tower, the Great Wall of China, the Taj Mahal, the Empire State Building, the Hollywood Sign, and more. "See?" he said. "Paris and LA are represented, but so is the rest of the world because I hope that we can see it all together."

"Finn . . ." she mumbled.

"You told me that you moved around a lot growing up, but that your mother made each new place feel like home by painting colorful murals on your bedroom walls."

"I can't believe you remembered that."

"Oh, this is the best part. Flip that switch," he said.

She flipped the switch, and the entire veranda was illuminated by twinkly lights. She smiled through her tears, sheer wonderment on her face.

"You also said your mother would string up twinkly lights." He paused for a moment and asked, "So, what do you think, sweetheart?"

She looked deeply into his eyes and said, "It's not a room; it's a love letter."

"I know you, Ella. Everything that matters. I love you with all my heart."

She wrapped her arms around him, holding him close, and whispered, "I love you." Eventually, she pulled back and said, "Come here. I know it's not what Lorraine intended, but let's go make good use of that couch."

FINN SIGHED DREAMILY, HIS LIMBS entwined with Ella's. "That was so beautiful," he whispered, kissing her softly.

"I feel so impossibly close to you," she said, tracing her finger along his eyebrow.

"Me too."

"Finn, when are we going to get married?"

He smiled. "I was waiting until you were ready. I'd marry you today, this instant. When should we do it?"

"The sooner, the better."

"We'll get back from my Boston film shoot by early September, so we could easily do it any time after that."

"How about the first of October?"

His face lit up. He kissed her again and said, "Let's do it. What kind of wedding do you want? Where should we have it?"

She shrugged. "I don't know. We can figure it out. The details are unimportant. All I know is that I love you and can't possibly live without you."

"Me too. The first of October it is," he said.

"I'm so excited. I have to tell my mother, to make sure she can come in from Spain. Do you mind if I call her?"

"Call her now! Tell her I'll send my jet and take care of everything. Then I'll call my parents."

"Okay," Ella replied, leaning down to retrieve her sundress from the floor. She pulled her cell phone out of the pocket and dialed her mother's number. "Hi, Mom. I'm calling . . . Yeah, Mom, that's great. But listen, I'm calling with news. We set the date for our wedding. We're getting married in October, on the first. You can make it, right? Finn said he'll take care of the arrangements . . . Yay! I can't wait for you and Alejandro to meet him." She glanced at Finn and he squeezed her shoulder, a wide smile across his face. "We can put you up at a hotel if you prefer, but there's plenty of room at Finn's house. Oh, Mom, wait until you see the office he created for me. It's magical. It's the most beautiful room in his house." Finn's heart sank, but Ella looked at him smiling and he smiled in return. "Okay, yes, we can go over all the details later. I just had to call and tell you right away. Tell Alejandro I said hi . . . Love you too. Bye."

She put her phone on the tea table and nuzzled into Finn, resting her head on his chest. He enfolded her in his arms, caressing her hair.

"I'm so happy. I can't believe this is all real," she said.

"Me too. Ella . . ."

"Yeah?" she asked, looking up into his eyes.

"I love you, that's all. Forever. I just want to make sure you know that."

She squeezed him tighter and said, "I love you too."

 **CHAPTER 6**

"**R**elax. Like I said before, she's adjusting," Michael said, inspecting his reflection in the mirror and smoothing his hair.

"Yeah, but by now . . ." Finn muttered.

"What?" Michael asked, picking up a bottle of hair spray and giving his coif a spritz.

"I had hoped that she would feel like it was her home by now. Every time she calls it 'Finn's house,' my heart breaks a little. The thought of losing her again is unbearable."

"Why don't you just talk to her about it?"

"I can't. Last time, I pushed her before she was ready, made her promise things she wasn't ready to say. I won't make that mistake again. It has to come from her. That's the only way it will feel real to both of us." He sighed heavily and added, "Her side of the closet is mostly empty, and there's a part of me that wonders if it's so she can make a break for it more easily, if she decides she can't do this."

"Ella never struck me as a clotheshorse. She probably doesn't give a shit about that kind of stuff."

"You're right," Finn said. "I'm probably just twisting myself into knots over nothing. Besides, she told me she had some shopping to do this week."

"Well, there you go."

Finn huffed. "It's funny. I couldn't care less about clothes or the Hollywood scene or any of that superficial junk. We're alike in that way. It's something I love about her. I don't know why this has even become something in my mind. It's like I've made it symbolic of something, but it's all just in my imagination."

"You're just a little on edge because of how she dumped you before," Michael said.

"Gee, thanks," Finn said.

"Sorry, that came out wrong. She set a date. That says everything you need to know."

Finn nodded. "You're right. I'm being ridiculous. Actually, she said she can't wait to get married."

"See, there you go. You're golden." Michael smoothed his hair one more time. "I just hope Lauren doesn't get any ideas when we're at your place tomorrow night. You know, about getting married."

"You love her, you live together, you have a kid. You really won't marry her?"

Michael shrugged. "I like to keep my options open."

Finn chuckled and shook his head. "We really are different creatures. There's nothing I want more than to know Ella and I will always be together."

"THANKS FOR COMING WITH ME," Ella said to Marni as they snaked through narrow pathways lined to the ceiling with bolts of fabric on either side. "I'm still learning how to get around in LA. This fabric shop is a gem. Look how beautiful these imported silks are."

"No problem. You're saving me from a meeting with a high-maintenance freelancer. There's nothing like a mid-morning escape from the office to clear one's head.

But tell me again, why the hell are you going to all this fuss? In my experience, no relationship is worth it."

"Well, Finn is worth it. Besides, you know how much I enjoy doing this kind of stuff."

"Yeah, but making your own chair cushions or slipcovers or whatever? Isn't that a bit much, even for you?" Marni asked. "The guy lives in a palace. Can't you have one of his minions do this?"

Ella smirked. "I'm meeting his closest friends for the first time, people I may be seeing for the rest of my life. I want it to feel like . . ."

"Like India?" Marni asked sarcastically, gesturing at the bolt of embellished fabric Ella was touching.

"No, I want it to feel like *me*." Ella paused and said, "Finn and I are building a life together. I want to bring all of me to it, the best of me. When I meet his friends, I hope we have some fun and really get to know each other. Creating the right atmosphere matters."

"And you're willing to go to the ends of the earth to make that happen?" Marni asked skeptically.

"I'm willing to go the extra mile, or in this case, to a fabric store in Venice Beach."

"Don't you have a book project you're supposed to be developing?"

"I will. Eventually," Ella replied.

"Just don't put your dreams on hold for some guy, even if he is your Prince Charming."

"I'm not. And he's hardly *some guy*," Ella retorted.

"I'll give you that. He's a bona fide movie star, and while I never use the word 'dashing,' it certainly fits the bill in this case."

Ella giggled. "What I meant is that he's the one I love. Love changes things."

"Just don't let it change you," Marni cautioned.

Ella huffed. "I used to be terrified of that. I'm not any-more. We even set the date for our wedding. Actually . . ." Before she could finish her thought, a bolt of fabric caught her eye. "Ooh, that one is perfect!"

THAT AFTERNOON, FINN CAME HOME and saw half a dozen large shopping bags in the living room. He beamed, think-ing Ella must have bought some clothes and her side of the closet would no longer be so bare. He followed the noise coming from the kitchen to find every countertop covered with mixing bowls and measuring cups, and Ella and Joyce cheerfully gabbing away. "What's all this?" he asked.

Ella looked up from the dough she was kneading, a streak of flour across her forehead. "Hi, love. We're just prepping things for tomorrow night."

He furrowed his brow in confusion.

"For the dinner party, silly," she explained.

"I thought we were doing a barbecue out back," he said.

"We are." Ella turned to Joyce and said, "Would you mind taking over for me for a minute? I want to show Finn everything I bought." She wiped her hands on a dish towel and took Finn's arm, leading him to the living room. "I've had the busiest couple of days, getting everything ready for tomorrow night."

"But baby, what about your next book? You wanted to start writing. I don't want to take time away from what's important to you."

"Meeting your friends is important to me," she replied. "Look at this incredible fabric. Isn't it stunning? I'm going to use it to create a runner down the center of the table," she said, emptying one of the large bags onto the couch. "Oh, and you have to see the colorful paper lanterns. Joyce said the gardeners can string them up over the table tomorrow," she added, sifting through the bags to find them.

"I don't understand why you bought all of this," he said forcefully.

She turned to him, a mixture of hurt and worry on her face. "I'm sorry," she said softly. "You told me I could use the credit card and . . ."

"No, baby, that's not what I mean. You can use it for absolutely anything you want. I just thought we were hosting a simple barbecue tomorrow night and that we'd have Joyce throw a few steaks on the grill and call it a day."

"When you suggested grilling, I came up with the perfect theme," Ella said, sounding excited again. "I'm calling it 'Morocco to Monaco.' I love the alliteration. Dinner will be a grilled Moroccan-inspired feast, and for dessert we're making two French tarts, which I figured we could eat around the firepit. Let me show you the take-away gifts," she continued, rifling through the bags again.

"Ella, I didn't intend for you to do all this work. I . . ."

"Oh, here they are," she said.

"Damn it, Ella! I didn't want any of this! It was supposed to be a simple barbecue!" he snapped.

Ella gasped. "I . . . I . . ." she stuttered as her eyes filled with tears. She would no longer meet his eyes.

"That's not what I meant, baby," Finn said, softening his voice. "I'm sorry. I only meant that I never wanted you to go to all this trouble."

"I need to go help Joyce," she murmured, walking away.

"Ella . . ." he called, but she didn't turn around.

He collapsed onto the couch and dropped his head into his hands, lost in a whirl of shame and remorse.

WHEN ELLA RETURNED TO THE KITCHEN, Joyce was hunched over a recipe book, reading some instructions. "So, it says . . ." She heard Ella sniffle and turned to look. "Oh, Ella, what's wrong, dear?"

"Finn isn't happy," she replied, choking back tears. "I guess he thinks this is all stupid or something."

"Oh, I'm sure he doesn't think that," Joyce said, wrapping her arms around her in a comforting embrace.

Ella hugged her for a long moment, sniffled, and composed herself. "I really should get back to the dough," she muttered, entirely deflated.

"How can I help?" Joyce asked.

A LITTLE WHILE LATER, FINN WENT TO the kitchen looking for Ella so he could properly apologize. He found Joyce cleaning up and asked, "Where's Ella?"

"We finished up for the day, and she said she was tired and wanted to rest."

"Thanks," Finn said, turning to leave.

"Finn?" Joyce called.

"Yes?" he replied, turning to her.

"I may be overstepping, but you once said that nothing was more important to you than Ella's happiness and that we should all do everything we can, and . . ."

"Please, speak freely," he said.

"Today was the happiest I've seen her since she moved here. She was having a ball. She was so excited for you to see everything."

Finn sighed.

"When she came back after speaking with you, she was crying."

He shuddered. "Thank you for telling me, Joyce."

With his head hung and his shoulders slumped, he went

upstairs to their bedroom and lightly tapped on the door before letting himself in. Ella was standing at the window, her back to him. "Ella," he said quietly.

She sniffled. "I'm sorry if I'm in your way. I was just coming to take a nap."

"You're not in my way," he said as he approached her. "You could never be in my way." He put his arms around her waist and whispered, "Sweetheart, I'm so sorry."

"Nothing I do pleases you," she said, bursting into tears.

"Oh, baby, that isn't true."

"My clothes, my car, even the way I throw a dinner party," she sputtered in between sobs. "To you, everything I do is wrong. Everything about me is wrong."

"Sweetheart, nothing could be further from the truth. I'm so sorry. I'm so sorry," Finn said, rubbing her back. "Please, baby. Let me see your eyes."

Ella turned to him, her face red and puffy. He used his thumbs to gently wipe the tears from under her eyes. He cupped her cheeks in his hands and softly said, "I was scared. I was scared out of my mind and I fucked up. I'm so sorry. Please let me try to explain." He guided her to the love seat, and they sat down together. They held each other and he rubbed her back, all the while whispering, "I'm so sorry."

Eventually, she pulled back, looked into his eyes, and said, "I was just trying to make things special for tomorrow night."

"I know, baby," he replied, caressing her cheek. "I panicked, thinking my life might be overtaking yours. I was afraid that if meeting my friends took too much energy, became too inconvenient, took time away from your work, then . . ."

"What?"

"You'd decide it was all too much and you might leave me."

"I would never leave you," she said.

"You already did."

"Oh, Finn." She took a deep breath and said, "That last morning we were together in Sweden, tearing myself out of bed, out of your arms, was the hardest, most agonizing thing I've ever done in my life. I loved you so much. I know I hurt you terribly, and I would give anything to take that away. I'm so sorry. There isn't a day that has passed that I haven't been filled with regret for leaving."

"It was my fault, Ella. It was all my fault."

"Finn, I was scared. It wasn't your fault, it was . . ."

"Baby, I know you've blamed yourself, and I shouldn't have let you. It was my fault. When we met, I didn't tell you I was seeing someone else. Letting you find out second-hand, how could I expect you to trust me after that?" She shook her head, but he stroked her cheek and continued. "I fell in love with you so deeply, so instantly. We had only known each other for a few days when I told you how I felt and asked you to tell me you were mine. Within a matter of weeks, I told you I wanted to marry you and pressured you to uproot your life to be with me. I knew it was a lot for you, but I pressed anyway. So many times, I could see you were trying to tell me it was too much, but I always interrupted you, brushed you off, or tried to steer the conversation back to how much we loved each other. You needed more time, and I should have given it to you. All that pain we both went through was my fault. I'm so sorry."

"Oh, Finn," she whispered, tears in her eyes.

He gently kissed her forehead. "Ella, when I look at you, I see my whole life—all the laughter, the joy, even our children who I already love even though they're only a dream. That's how much you mean to me." Tears slid silently down her cheeks. "When we got back together and you moved here, I promised myself that I would do everything right this time, that I would give you the space to be who you are. When I saw all the effort you're going through for tomorrow night, I thought I had done it again, allowed my life and desires to overtake yours."

She rested her forehead against his and whispered, "I love you so much."

"I love you too. More than anything in the world."

She pulled back and said, "I always loved you, more than I can say. I just wasn't ready then. At the time, I thought it was because some part of me didn't trust you or trust that what we had would last, but it was more than that. It wasn't you I didn't trust, it was me, and maybe even love itself. I was afraid that if I fully gave myself to you, that I'd somehow change, that I'd lose myself. Then if you weren't there one day, I'd be left with nothing. But Finn, that fear is long gone." She touched his cheek. "The truth is, I have no idea what love is like over a lifetime, but I want to find out, and I want to do that with you. I trust what we have, body and soul." He smiled and she continued, "It seems you've forgotten what I told you on the jet, so I'm going to give you a reminder. I choose you. I choose us. Always."

"Oh, baby, I love you so much," he said, kissing her tenderly. "I'm so sorry I raised my voice. I'm so sorry about everything."

"I'll never leave you again. I want to be here with you. But I need to be myself."

"That's what I want too."

"As for the dinner party, it wasn't any trouble at all. When we were in Sweden, I told you how much I love entertaining and about all the get-togethers I used to throw. Your life wasn't overtaking mine. I was trying to bring myself to your life, to our life."

"That's so sweet."

"I know maybe you think the theme is silly, but . . ."

"I don't think that at all," Finn assured her. "I love it."

"It's an icebreaker. It gives people something to talk about and makes it easier to get to know one another."

"How about a date night at home with your future husband? Takeout of your choice, maybe a bubble bath, and you can tell me everything about tomorrow night, like how you came up with the fantastic idea of Morocco to Monaco. What do you say?"

Ella smiled brightly. "I say yes."

THE NEXT DAY, JUST BEFORE THEIR guests were set to arrive at six o'clock, Finn wandered out back, wearing jeans and a black T-shirt. His eyes marveled when he saw the spectacularly set dining table: hot-pink, gold-trimmed slip cushions on each chair, an ornate turquoise-and-gold runner down the center of the table, white plates atop gold chargers with matching gold flatware, beautifully folded emerald-green napkins, bud vases brimming with white flowers, and a sprinkling of glowing votive candles, all beneath a canopy of brightly colored paper lights. He was so captivated by how Ella was present in every detail that he didn't hear her approach.

"Hey, you," she said.

He turned and watched her walk toward him, her turquoise sundress and long spiral curls blowing in the breeze. "You are breathtaking. The table is stunning. Creative, magical, and one of a kind, just like you."

She blushed and gave him a smooch. "Everything is all set in the kitchen. I thought we could have cocktails and chat when everyone arrives. Joyce and her assistant will grill the meats and veggies, and then we can eat."

"Okay, baby."

An hour later, they all sat down to dinner, Finn and Ella at the opposite heads of the table. Their guests were chatting with one another about the eye-catching place settings, admiring every detail.

"I'd like to make a toast," Finn said, raising his wine glass. "To Ella, for creating this very special evening, and to all of you for joining us."

"Cheers!" everyone said.

Ella smiled and said, "Let me explain what's on the table. These round breads are called *khobz*, and you can use them like pita. Fill it with whatever you like and fold it over like a pocket—there's marinated lamb, beef, chicken, and vegetables. Play around with the sauces; the green is zesty herbs, the red one is spicy, and the white is a yogurt cucumber sauce, which is mild and cooling. There's couscous and salads as well. Dig in."

The guests began piling their plates. "Oh, wow," Carol moaned. "Honey, you have to try the lamb with the green sauce," she said to her husband.

"This bread is killer. I could spend the whole night dipping it in these sauces until I burst," Dan said.

Finn sat back and smiled, unabashed joy on his face.

After taking seconds and thirds, everyone was finally finished eating. Lauren picked up the snow globe behind her place setting and asked, "Ella, what's this?"

"Everyone has a snow globe that represents a different destination—there's Paris, Rome, Shanghai, Bali, Sydney, Tokyo, Abu Dhabi, and Rio de Janeiro. They're your take-home gifts. Check out which one you got. Maybe it will inspire you to think about the places you've visited or to dream up new ideas."

"I got Paris," Lauren said, shaking her snow globe and watching as the sparkles drifted down over the Eiffel Tower. She looked at Michael and said, "I've never been. I can only imagine that it's as wonderful as everyone says."

"Well, maybe we'll have to plan a little trip sometime," he replied, draping his arm around her and kissing her cheek.

Ella smiled at them and said, "It's beautiful and so romantic. You should go. I loved living there."

"How'd you end up there?" Dan asked.

"It was happenstance, I suppose. I was living in New York but itching for a change. My friend Jean invited me to visit him in Paris. He was heading into a divorce, so I went to support him. Fell madly in love with the city—the art, the culture, the energy. We were out to dinner one night with a group of Jean's friends, and one of them mentioned that she was looking to sublet her apartment while she took a job in London. Jean whispered, 'Ella, *ma chérie*, you should take it. Paris suits you.' I was getting ready to write four short books about pleasure, each on a different topic. One was going to be about food, and it seemed like if I were going to spend months overeating, Paris would be a good place to do it. So, I moved."

"That's so cool," Lauren said. "I love how you take chances like that and live so freely. I've barely left California."

Ella smiled. "I've always had a bit of wanderlust."

"Do you think you've finally gotten that out of your system?" Michael asked, glancing at Finn out of the corner of his eye.

"I hope not. Finn and I both love to travel. I hope we have a lifetime of grand adventures together. After all, birds build nests but they still fly." She and Finn exchanged a smile, their eyes lingering on each other. After a moment passed, she asked, "So, who else wants to share their snow globe?"

"I got Australia. I've always wanted to go to the Great Barrier Reef for a scuba diving trip. Has anyone ever done that?" Jim asked.

"We did. It's incredible beyond words. If you're going to go, I have some recommendations. We made a few mistakes when we went," Tom said.

"We sure did," Elise chimed in, patting his arm. "For starters, you should actually know how to scuba before you let some random guy take you out on an expedition."

Everyone laughed.

"This one was like, 'I'm athletic, it's no problem.' He was singing a different tune as he lay on the floor of the boat, thanking the universe that he'd survived."

"Ooh, that reminds me of the time we were in Greece and ended up on this crazy donkey ride because we misread the tour sign," Chuck said. "My back hurt for weeks."

They all cracked up.

"I've always wanted to go to Greece. Were you on the mainland?" Lauren asked.

"We spent most of our time in the Greek Isles, on Santorini. The beaches are everything you'd imagine and more."

"Just don't go to Lesvos," Ella warned. "I tagged along with a friend who got a free trip to speak at a conference. Packed my entire suitcase with bathing suits only to discover it's the only island in Greece without sandy beaches. There were stray dogs everywhere too. We spent most of our time sitting at a little British pub that oddly had the best food on the island. Basically, my brief experience of Greece was eating shepherd's pie and fending off dogs that looked more like coyotes."

Finn laughed so hard he had to hold his stomach, and the others joined in.

The boisterous conversation continued, but all the while, Finn couldn't take his eyes off Ella. Over an hour later, Ella said, "Everyone get comfortable around the firepit while I run to the kitchen to get the dessert. I hope you saved room. We have an almond apricot tart with amaretto whipped cream, and because Finn is a chocoholic, there's also a spicy chocolate tart with cinnamon whipped cream."

Finn grazed Ella's arm as she brushed past him to head inside. The group plopped down into Adirondack chairs. As soon as they were seated, Dan and Jim started clapping. "Dude, she's a goddess," Dan said. "Does she have any single friends exactly like her?" Finn blushed, an irrepressible smile on his face.

The others echoed the sentiments. "You must be the most eligible bachelor in the world and one of the greatest guys we know. We all wondered who would eventually snag you," Carol said. "Ella is fantastic."

"That she is," Finn agreed.

After they said good night to their last guest, who raved that it was the best dinner party he had ever attended, Ella said, "Your friends are great. It was so nice of the gals to invite me to join their book club. Now I have two groups to hang out with."

"Come here, love," Finn said, taking her hand and guiding her upstairs. Once inside their bedroom oasis, he couldn't stop staring at her, his hands on her waist. He looked at her with total adoration, searching for the words to express the depth of what he was feeling. Eventually, he said, "You are spectacular, Ella Sinclair. Who you are, the way you do things, how you make people feel, how you make me feel—it's so very special. I love everything about the life we're creating, and I love you with all my heart."

She kissed him. "Ravage me all night."

THE NEXT MORNING AT BREAKFAST, Ella tapped on the shell of her soft-boiled egg. "There really is something so satisfying about that sound. Do you remember that first breakfast we had together in Sweden?"

"It was the first time we were ever alone. I remember every word," Finn said.

"I told you about the four books I was writing about pleasure, and the idea of oneness I have. You asked if I had considered writing about love."

"You said it was too abstract a concept."

She smiled. "It is, but I've decided to tackle it. It's going to be my next project, a philosophical exploration of love. It'll probably take me forever, but I'm ready for a big challenge."

"That's great, sweetheart."

"I was always afraid of what happens to our identities, to our sense of being whole on our own when we truly love another. Albie knew about my fear and tried to nudge me in the right direction. When we were all leaving Sweden, he told me love is all that matters. He said, 'Love, Ella. Love.' I've never been able to get those words out of my mind." He smiled and she continued, "Finn, last night I was thinking . . ." Ella was interrupted when her cell phone rang, and she retrieved it from her pocket. "Ah, it's Marni. She's probably calling to see how the dinner went." She answered the call. "Hey, Marni . . . It was perfect. His friends are great . . . Well sure, that's no problem. We can have the meeting at my place." Finn had to catch his breath. He tried to maintain a straight face as Ella finished her call, but he couldn't mask his smile. "Okay, bye," she said.

"Having your next philosophy club meeting here?" he asked.

"Uh-huh. Jade's still having roommate issues. What's that grin for?"

"That was the first time you referred to our home as yours. I'm so happy you're feeling comfortable here."

"Last night was so much fun, and I finally felt like I could truly be myself here. I feel like I belong." He rubbed her hand and she continued, "In fact, before we were interrupted by the phone, I was going to say that the backyard is such a beautiful place to entertain. I was thinking that maybe we should have our wedding here. We could have a tent set up. It would be nice to get married here in our home. What do you think?"

Finn smiled so widely he could barely speak. "That would be perfect."

 **CHAPTER 7**

"Dante texted that he and Jade are both running late. Gives us a chance to catch up. So, Miss Soon-to-Be-Married, how was Boston?" Marni asked.

"Fantastic. The studio rented us the most charming Victorian house in Cambridge, right off Brattle Street near Harvard Square. Finn would go to work and I'd wander down to this little Middle Eastern café, drink fresh mint tea, and read and write for hours. I also connected with some folks at Harvard and MIT to discuss their research and how it relates to my work. On Finn's days off, we went sightseeing all over the city and had romantic dinners in the North End and on the Seaport. I especially loved all the old brownstones and antique shops on Charles Street. We even drove to Cape Cod for a couple of nights and gorged ourselves on steamers and lobster."

"It's cool that you can travel with him to locations. You've always been a road dog. I know it helps to fuel your work."

"Yeah. Finn and I made a deal that we'd always travel together and make an adventure of life. When we have children, we'll travel as a family and experience the world together. Once our oldest is school-age, Finn promised to only take jobs in LA except for in the summers, when we can all travel together."

"Seems he really is the perfect guy for you," Marni said.

"He is," Ella said, smiling.

"You know me, I find it hard to believe in the whole knight-in-shining-armor thing. I always wonder if they're really just a Trojan horse. So, if it's all the same to you, I'll hang on to a healthy dose of skepticism."

Ella laughed. "Suit yourself. My worry is that my mother may share the same sentiment. She and her boyfriend arrive in LA tonight. Finn arranged for them to have a spa day tomorrow to unwind after their trip, then we're taking them out to dinner where everyone will meet for the first time."

"I remember Carmen being very warm and free-spirited—boho, like you. Isn't romantic love right up her whimsical alley?"

"Lust, yes. Love, maybe. Marriage, not so much. I think she's happy for me, but . . ."

Marni raised her eyebrows.

"I need to prepare Finn in case she says something off-putting. It's just another ball to keep in the air. You can't imagine what a jumble my mind is with the wedding in only three days. There's so much to do, and I just want everything to go off without a hitch."

"It will," Marni assured her. "I may not be the most romantic of hearts, but you are and Finn is, and that's all that matters."

"Thanks."

"But with everything you have going on, why did you come to our meeting today?"

"I missed the last couple of months because of the shoot, and after the wedding, we'll be honeymooning on the Amalfi Coast for two weeks. I don't want to get kicked out of the group for truancy."

"Fat chance. You know I've always had a fondness for delinquents."

Ella laughed. "Besides, before I get married, I wanted a little reminder of who I am. Just me."

Marni smiled. "Well, I may not have the bridal gene in me, but I'm happy for you. To show it, I plan to get rip-roaring drunk at the wedding."

"Do me a favor: if my mother needs it, get her drunk too."

"HEY, SWEETHEART. THE JET LANDED and your mother and Alejandro are being driven to their hotel," Finn said.

"Thank you again for taking care of all the arrangements."

"My pleasure. Are you sure you wouldn't rather have them stay here? There's plenty of room."

"My mother thought we should have privacy this of all weeks," Ella explained. "But maybe after dinner tomorrow, we could invite them over for a nightcap and to see the house, if they're not too jet-lagged."

"Sure."

"And then they're still planning to come over the night before the wedding for dinner with us and your parents."

"Are you sure they really want to cook?" Finn asked. "It's not too late to have Joyce handle it."

"It's their way; they love to feed people Spanish food. We bought all the ingredients so they can make their famous saffron paella and squid ink paella."

"My parents will love it. I picked up a few special bottles of Rioja to go with dinner."

"Thank you."

He noticed her fidgeting with her hair, so he asked, "Is everything okay, sweetheart? You seem nervous. Not cold feet, I hope."

Ella smiled. "Not in the slightest. I'm just a little anxious about seeing my mother."

"I always had the impression you two are close."

"We are. Very close. The whole single mother and daughter thing is tough to explain, but we were kind of everything to each other—family and best friends. It's just . . ."

"What? Tell me."

"I want you to like each other." She took a moment to consider her words. "I've only ever said good things about you, but I visited her in Valencia about a month after Sweden, and I wasn't exactly doing well at the time. I told her how much I wanted to get back together with you, and . . ." He smiled and rubbed her hand. "She wasn't exactly optimistic that it would work out."

"Given the situation at the time, I can understand that. Surely now she can see that it has worked out."

Ella sighed. "I hope so. To her, maybe it's a little like a fairy tale and it's hard for her to believe it's real. My mother doesn't have a lot of faith in marriage. She doesn't think it lasts, which is why she's never been married. After her affair with my father, the way he strung her along and then bailed on us both . . ."

"Don't worry," Finn said, taking her hand. "I'll do everything I can to show her how committed I am to you, even if I have to spend the next fifty years proving myself to her."

Ella smiled. "She's happy for me, really. I'm just not totally sure how she feels about us getting married. I've been afraid to go there with her."

"As long as you know how *you* feel about it, everything else will work itself out."

"I do."

"Just make sure you remember those two little words for our wedding day."

She giggled.

FINN PULLED UP TO THE CURB IN front of Avra and noticed several paparazzi standing outside the restaurant. He turned to Ella and said, "This is the price of eating in Beverly Hills. I'm sorry in advance. Don't get out until I come around to get you. We can zip inside." The valet opened their doors, and Finn came around and took Ella's hand. They ducked their heads and hurried inside, paparazzi snapping away and hollering, "When's the big day?"

Before they could say a word, the hostess said, "Good evening, Mr. Forrester. Your party is already here; please follow me." She escorted them straight past the bar, up a few stairs, and into a private room that could easily seat a party several times their size.

"Mom!" Ella called as she made her way to the table. Carmen and Alejandro both rose and hugged her affectionately. "Mom, Alejandro, this is Finn."

"I'm so pleased to meet you," Finn said, extending his hand. "I see where Ella gets her beauty. You look so much alike, like sisters."

Carmen smiled, leaned in, and gave him a peck on each cheek. "Well, you certainly are charming. It's a pleasure to finally meet you."

Finn and Alejandro shook hands, and they all sat down.

"I hope the hotel is okay. How have you been settling in?" Finn asked.

"Very well, thank you. The suite is lovely, and we enjoyed a relaxing day at the spa. Thank you for taking care of everything for us. We feel positively spoiled," Carmen said.

Finn smiled. "We know it's a long trip for you, but it means so much to us that you're here for our big day. We want you to enjoy yourselves."

"We wouldn't have missed it," Alejandro added in his thick accent. "As Carmen said, thank you for the luxurious accommodations. This seems like a wonderful restaurant too; I love Mediterranean food. The fish they have displayed in the other room looks supremely fresh. Very European to serve whole fish, so I feel right at home."

"Ella mentioned you both enjoy seafood," Finn said.

"Yes," Carmen replied. "Although I'm not sure why they insisted on seating us back here where we can't see the fish market."

"Mom, sometimes Finn gets unwanted attention, so he reserved this room special for us," Ella explained.

"I hope you don't mind. I thought we could use a little privacy while we get to know each other," Finn said.

Carmen huffed. "Privacy? I'm surprised that's important to you considering you're the man who proposed to my daughter in the middle of the most famous red carpet in the world, in front of swarms of onlookers and the international media. One might wonder what your intentions were: marriage or simply a grand moment?"

"Mom," Ella cautioned.

"I'm sorry," Carmen said. "That came out wrong."

"Not at all," Finn said. "I greatly value my privacy, but I had just fallen so hopelessly in love with your remarkable daughter that when I finally had the chance to propose, I couldn't stop myself, red carpet or not. To tell you the truth, I didn't even notice that anyone else was there. My eyes only saw Ella."

Alejandro patted Carmen's hand, and a smile flickered across her face.

"Ah, love. The greatest gift in the world," Alejandro remarked.

"It sure is," Finn agreed, draping his arm around his bride-to-be.

Just then, a waiter came over and asked, "Can I start you off with something to drink?"

"Should we order a bottle of wine?" Finn asked.

"Perhaps a bottle of champagne. I wish to toast the happy occasion of my daughter's engagement," Carmen said.

Finn smiled, looked at the waiter, and said, "A bottle of your best champagne, please."

Two hours later, they were laughing at Ella's story about a sex shop she visited as research for her book. "Do you mind?" Alejandro asked, gesturing at the last piece of grilled octopus.

"Please, help yourself," Finn replied. "It was a great idea to order a bunch of dishes to share. The sashimi you selected was fantastic, and so was the grilled vegetable and Halloumi plate."

Alejandro scooped up the last piece of octopus and said, "That is how we like to do it in Spain—small bites and a whole fish to share, and everyone gets a little of everything, family style, as you Americans say."

"Yes, I've quite acclimated to the Spanish way after all these years," Carmen said.

"How did you end up in Valencia?" Finn asked.

"Well, I joke that with a name like Carmen, I was destined to live in Spain."

"Lucky for me," Alejandro said, picking up her hand and kissing it.

"Anyway," Carmen continued, "I've always moved around a lot, as I'm sure Ella told you, although I tried to stay in the States when she was growing up to make it easier for her in school. About ten years ago, Ella's first book had just come out. It seemed she was truly an adult out in the world on her own, and that gave me the freedom to go wherever I pleased. Europe beckoned, preferably somewhere with a warm climate. I was considering Barcelona, but a friend suggested that Valencia might be an easier place to live and boasts a vibrant arts community. I decided to try it for a year or two, but it suited me so well that I stuck around. A decade later, it feels like home."

"I like to think I have something to do with that," Alejandro said.

"How did you two meet?" Finn asked.

"He rented me my apartment. I mentioned that I was looking for a place with good light for my painting. So, he invited me to a local café where artists share their work—guitar, spoken word, poetry. I stopped by, and to my surprise, he was on stage, reading the most beautiful poetry."

"A real estate manager by day, but a poet in my soul," Alejandro mused. "It took me ages to get her to go out with me and years more before she agreed to live with me. These Sinclair women are tough." Finn laughed and Alejandro continued, "Wrote poem after poem for her, professing my love. In the end, I won her over with my art."

Finn smiled.

"Yes, the arts can be quite an aphrodisiac," Carmen said. "They can make the impossible seem possible. A gift and a curse. You two must relate. After all, you met on an exotic film location. I'm sure that makes it easy to get swept up in the romance of it all."

"I've spent my life on movie sets but never felt a glimmer of the jolt I got when I met Ella. I think when you meet the one, it's inexplicable. You just know it. Then it's up to you to lean in."

"I think so too," Ella said, gazing at him.

Carmen watched them and smiled softly. "Yes, perhaps."

"AH, HAVE YOU FINISHED THE TOUR of the house?" Finn asked as Carmen wandered into the living room.

She nodded. "They're still in Ella's office. Alejandro is like a kid in a candy store flipping through the first-edition poetry books you bought her. Truthfully, I snuck away because I was hoping to speak with you alone."

He handed her a glass of port and said, "Please, have a seat."

"Thank you," she replied as they sat on the couch.

"Cheers," he said, clinking his glass to hers.

They each took a sip, and Carmen set her glass on the coffee table. "Finn, I feel I owe you an apology. I was a little hard on you."

"Not at all. You're just looking out for your daughter. I realize it will take some time for us to get to know each other. I'm hoping that life is long and I'll have the chance to prove myself and the depth of my devotion."

She smiled. "Did Ella tell you she came to see me shortly after you two split up?"

"Yes."

"Did she tell you what I said?"

He shook his head. "Only that you were a bit skeptical that it would work out."

"Ella was an absolute wreck. She couldn't stop crying, days on end. I've never seen her like that before. She said she was madly in love with you. I told her that passionate love affairs may not be meant to last and she would need to come to peace with it as a cherished memory. She said she wasn't sure if she could do that." Carmen stopped, shook her head, and continued, "I told her that you're a movie star, that you probably fall in and out of love at every location, and it was all too good to be true. You hadn't called her since leaving Sweden, so I tried to convince her that you had moved on."

"There wasn't a moment that passed that I wasn't thinking of Ella. I didn't reach out because I knew it had to come from her. I wanted to spend the rest of my life with her. I knew we belonged together, that what we share is a once-in-a-lifetime kind of love. She needed the time and space to figure that out for herself."

She smiled. "I know. I also know that the reason she left you in the first place has as much to do with me as anything else."

Finn looked at her quizzically.

"My lifestyle wasn't easy on her, always moving around."

"Perhaps, but she also said that you made each new place feel like home. 'Oodles of joy' were her words. You also taught her to have an adventurous spirit, which is something I adore about her."

"You're kind to say that," Carmen said. "I did my best, given who I am. When Ella showed me the mural you had painted for her and the twinkly lights on her balcony, it was clear to me how she remembered her childhood, the good and the bad. It was also clear how deeply you love her."

"I do. I love her with all my heart. I always will."

"Ella had a hard time allowing herself to fall in love because of my relationship with her father, the other men who came and went, my lifestyle before Alejandro. I'm sorry for my role in what you both went through and for not making the road back to each other easier."

"Please, Carmen, you have absolutely nothing to apologize for. You raised the love of my life. Ella is the most extraordinary woman I've ever known. There's nothing I would change about her. It's clear she takes after you in many ways."

Carmen smiled. "I see how much you and Ella love each other, and I'm truly happy for you both. Perhaps for some, fairy tales do come true and passionate love can last a lifetime. That's my wish for the two of you."

Finn smiled, and Ella and Alejandro ambled into the room.

"Ella and I got swept up reading poetry. It's easy to get lost in the beauty of the Romantics and their hopefulness," Alejandro said.

"So, what have we missed?" Ella asked.

"I guess your groom and I were having our own chat about the beauty of hopefulness. Let's just say, he's made me a believer," Carmen said, winking at Finn.

"GOOD MORNING, LOVE," ELLA SAID, running her finger down Finn's cheek. "I can't believe our wedding day is here."

"Me too," he said, smiling. "It's already the happiest day of my life."

"Mine too. I hope my wedding dress still fits. We were pretty indulgent last night."

"That paella was amazing. My parents loved your mother and Alejandro; it seems like they could have talked all night. I even heard them mention taking a trip together."

"I started to wonder if we'd have to throw them all out so we could get some sleep."

He laughed. "I'm just grateful everyone gets along so well."

"Me too. You certainly dazzled my mother. I wasn't sure if it could be done, but once she let her guard down, she could see what an incredible man you are and how we truly feel about each other. She's so happy for us." Ella got quiet for a moment.

"What is it, my love?" Finn asked.

"She offered to walk me down the aisle. Alejandro did too. Jean even texted me when his jet landed yesterday to offer the same. He said, '*Ma chérie*, since I am responsible for you and Finn meeting, I would be honored to walk you to him if you need an escort. Besides, it would be my first stroll down the aisle that had any chance of working out.'"

Finn laughed.

"I guess they all feel badly that I don't have a father to walk me," she said.

He ran the back of his hand along her cheek. "I'm sorry, baby. Does the wedding have you thinking about your father leaving you?"

"Not really. If anything, it makes me think about how lucky I am to have a man in my life who will always love me."

He kissed her forehead. "So, what have you decided? Who's going to escort you?"

"No one. Today is about us. I want to walk to you on my own, my eyes glued to yours." He smiled and she continued, "My bridal bouquet is going to be tied with a white silk ribbon, like the one on that teddy bear my father gave me the last time I saw him, when I was four years old. It's my way of having him there, and also of letting go."

Finn kissed the tip of her nose. "Everything about you is so beautiful. I can't wait to marry you. Speaking of which, I know you wanted to buck tradition and sleep in our bed together last night . . ."

"After our separation, I can't bear to be apart from you."

He smiled. "But we also said we'd each go to different parts of the house today to get ready so we won't see each other until you're walking down the aisle to me. I'll be the guy in the tux who can't stop smiling."

"Finn . . ." She looked down, contemplative.

He touched her chin and raised her gaze to meet his. "What is it, love? You're not having second thoughts, are you?"

"Never. There's nothing I have ever wanted more than to be with you forever. Can we make a pact that no matter what, we'll keep our relationship at the center of our lives? I think that's an important part of making love last, and why it doesn't work out for some people when they add in the stresses of work and family. As much as we love our work, and how immeasurably we'll love our children, you and I, this thing between us," she said, touching his chest, "it will always come first."

"Yes, it's a pact."

"In my heart, I know that's how we can make it work, make it last."

"I feel the same way." He put his hand on her cheek and said, "I know you've always been afraid that if you gave yourself fully and vulnerably to someone, that you might lose yourself. I promise I'll never let that happen."

Ella smiled. "I promise the same to you." She kissed him and continued, "When we say our vows, there will be so many people watching us. It feels a bit strange, since it's the most personal, intimate thing we could ever do. I was thinking that maybe we could say something to each other now, while we're alone, something private and just for us. It can be our secret, real wedding. It doesn't have to be formal vows, maybe just something authentic about how we feel and what we want for our life together."

"I love that idea."

"I'll go first," she said. She traced his jawline with her finger. "Finn Forrester, I love you, body and soul, and I always will. I promise to spend the rest of my life loving you fearlessly with everything I have. My hope is that we live a passionate, adventurous life together—working, traveling, raising a family, and just being *us*. I want you to be my partner, now and forever. I trust what we have. And because of you, I trust love. I don't know what love looks like or feels like over a lifetime, I don't know what it will do to me or to you, but I want to find out. My heart is wide-open and yours for the rest of my days."

"My beautiful Ella," he said, cupping her cheek in his hand. "You are my world. I love you with all my heart. Together, we can live an adventure of our own making, and I can't wait to see how it unfolds. I know you'll keep me on my toes. I'm not perfect and I may make mistakes, but I will never betray or abandon you. I'm yours, completely yours. When all else fails, remember this: I choose you. I choose us. Always."

 CHAPTER 8

"Wait, I want to carry my bride over the threshold," Finn said when the driver dropped them off at their estate.

"You've been doing that since our wedding night. We've been married for over two weeks already."

"Just this one last time," he promised, picking her up. "It's tradition."

Ella giggled and wrapped her arms around his neck. "If the most handsome man in the world wants to take me in his tanned, muscular arms, who am I to argue?"

He stepped inside and gently put her down, giving her a kiss. "Welcome home, Mrs. Ella Sinclair Forrester."

"Our honeymoon was beyond my wildest fantasies," Ella gushed. "The Amalfi Coast is spectacular. The color of the water, how it felt to float in it, splashing around with you—it was pure paradise. That house you rented us, I don't even have the words. Positively heavenly."

"It was the most magical time of my life, being alone with you in that beautiful setting. The best part of all was watching you run around topless on our private beach, so carefree and at peace. God, you're sexy." She blushed and he continued, "It's no wonder I had to have you over and over again."

"The feeling was mutual. Everything was so romantic. But then again, it always is with you," she said, running a finger down his cheek. "As if that trip weren't enough, I still can't believe you bought us a house in France. It's the most extraordinary wedding present, but you didn't have to be so extravagant. All I want is you."

"Ever since that night in Sweden when you told me you pictured us having a little vacation place in France where you could write and our kids could roll around in the grass, it's become my dream too." She glanced down. Finn touched her chin and pulled her eyes up to meet his. "Don't worry, love. I know we're not ready for a family yet. All I want is to be with you and let our life unfold, one adventure at a time." She smiled softly and he added, "As difficult as it was to leave our Italian oasis, I'm glad to be here in our home, married."

"Me too. That escape came at the perfect time. The next few months will be hectic. My North American book tour will be here before we know it. Are you still sure you can come with me?"

"I wouldn't miss it. My next film doesn't start shooting for a few months, so I'm all yours. We'll have a blast, jetting from city to city. I'm no scholar, but it's clear you've taken the philosophy world by storm. The attention and reviews you've received are well deserved. Your books are brave, unapologetic, and so forward-thinking. Amazing," he said, shaking his head in awe. "I'm looking forward to sitting in the audience each night, basking in the glow of my brilliant wife. After all, I am your biggest fan."

Ella giggled. "After the tour wraps, I'll need to dive into my new book in earnest. I have a notebook filled with ideas, but I'm still not quite sure how to tackle this project. Love feels like such an expansive, abstract topic. It's hard to capture it all, to find a centerpiece. I'll need to buckle down." He kissed her forehead and she continued, "And with all the accolades *Celebration* received, awards season will be upon us in the blink of an eye: the Golden Globes in January, the SAGs in February, and then we'll fly to London for the BAFTAs. It's just so wonderful that they're honoring Albie with the Lifetime Achievement Award. I only wish he were here to see the success of both the film and our relationship. Jean wants us all to go to dinner the night before to catch up and celebrate. Before you know it, the Oscars will be upon us."

"You've really got the awards season schedule down. I'm impressed," Finn said.

"Well, I am your wife now. I suppose I have to do my part to keep up your leading man status." He laughed and she continued, "Jason schooled me, told me about everything you'll be expected to attend. He's coming over tomorrow afternoon to talk designer gowns and borrowed jewels."

"Baby, I know how you feel about that stuff. If he's bothering you, I . . ."

"Not at all," she replied, giving his bicep a squeeze. "We're partners, you and I. Throwing on something sparkly to accompany my movie star husband to an awards ceremony is hardly a big sacrifice. Plus, I have a few surprises in store for Jason. I don't intend to lose my personal style."

Finn smiled. "Sweetheart, just be yourself. Don't worry about anything else. Whether we're on the red carpet in front of the media or locked away alone in our home, I'm the luckiest guy in the world. Now that I've gotten hold of you, the last thing I want is for you to lose yourself."

"Well, maybe you could help me lose myself in another way," she said with a mischievous glint in her eyes. "How about you carry me over the threshold one more time? But this time, carry me into our bedroom. After all, it's tradition."

"ELLA, I WAS SO EXCITED YOU TOOK me up on my offer," Jason said as he laid an armful of garment bags on the bed. "I've brought over some of my top picks, but don't worry, there are many more options where these came from. We can always go custom too. Every designer in town is vying for the chance to dress you. They expect that you'll get massive press coverage, both television and print. They're not wrong."

Ella furrowed her brow. "You can't be serious. I'm not even a celebrity."

"Uh, yes, you are. Ever since your appearance on the red carpet in Cannes with Finn down on bended knee, you're the toast of Tinseltown. As far as Hollywood is concerned, you and Finn are *the* It Couple. In fact, there's no one the world is more eager to see arm in arm and doing the glamorous power-couple sashay than you two. It's like a real-life fairy tale, you and Finn. People love it."

"Really?"

He nodded. "Besides, and I hope Finn doesn't fire me for saying this, you're more beautiful than any actress I've ever seen. It's no wonder everyone is so fascinated by your love story."

"That's sweet, but . . ."

"I know this is all new to you. That's what I'm here for. This is a big year for Finn; it looks like he'll be nominated for lead actor across the board. You'll both need to look the part. Shall I start showing you the gowns?"

"Before we get into that, I thought we could have a little chat since we're still getting to know each other. I realize it's your job to make sure the carriage doesn't turn into a pumpkin in public view, but I don't need you to bibbidi-bobbidi-boo me."

Jason laughed. "Got it, no fairy dust."

"I appreciate that this is all part of Finn's life," she said, gesturing at the garment bags, "and I'm willing to play the glam game for his benefit. That said, I'm not interested in what the world thinks about our relationship, nor am I concerned with fulfilling some sort of collective fantasy. I simply want to support my husband."

"I hear you loud and clear. Tell me what you need."

"I want to do this my way, and I'd like your help."

CHAPTER 9

When Finn and Ella arrived at the famed Ivy restaurant, the hostess recognized them immediately. "The rest of the Mercier party is here," she said, escorting them to a table in the far corner with a view of the bustling room and elegant, mirrored bar.

Jean, Willow, Charlotte, and Michael jumped up to greet them.

"*Ma chérie*, you look radiant as always," Jean said, giving her a kiss on each cheek. "We took the liberty of ordering your drinks."

"Thanks. You were sweet to pick this restaurant. Reminds me of the first night we met, all those years ago," Ella replied. "Sorry we're late. The London traffic never ceases. It's so great to see you all," she said, hugging each of their friends.

"So, have you been enjoying London?" Charlotte asked as they took their seats.

"We got here two days ago," Finn replied. "Figured we'd make the most of it. We spent yesterday in Notting Hill. Ella's mad for old books, so we went roaming around the rare and used bookshops, where she found a few treasures. Then we had a romantic dinner in a little booth at Berners Tavern."

"They have the best steak and fish and chips, so we splurged and shared a bit of each. Today, we went to Tate Modern. They have the most fascinating exhibit on surrealism. I adore how I can always count on the surrealists to find beauty in the unlikeliest of places and to push people to think beyond their comfort zones. You would have loved it," Ella said, looking at Jean.

He smirked. "The surrealists turned things on their head because they weren't afraid to explore the dark side, searching for a hint of something beautiful in the vast wasteland of human ugliness and despair."

"Tell us what you really think," Ella said with a giggle.

"It's a bleak abyss. The human species is dark and depraved," he said, taking a swill of his drink.

"I do love how French you are," Ella said.

Finn burst into laughter.

Jean shrugged. "Artists must be truth tellers. No reason to sugarcoat it."

"And you wonder why the press has called you dystopian," Ella mused.

Finn and Michael laughed, and Charlotte and Willow couldn't help but join in.

"Yes, well, the surrealists have served as fuel for my work. The inspiration for many of my films no doubt comes from the unconscious. It's one of the reasons my scripts are so sparse, so that the scenes can unfold naturally, just as our thoughts, our dreams, our nightmares do," Jean explained.

"Here I always thought you were just a lazy writer," Ella said.

Finn and Michael exploded with laughter, and Charlotte demurely covered her mouth.

"Say what you will, but there must be a method to my madness. After all, Willow here has already won the Golden

Globe and SAG award for her role in *Celebration*. Seems the Oscar may be next."

Willow blushed as the others started hooting and hollering.

"You guys," she said, looking down.

"I remember how nervous you were when we started filming," Charlotte said. "You did a magnificent job. It's lovely to see how your career has taken off."

"Thank you. I never thought I'd have the chance for a fresh start or the kinds of opportunities that are coming my way. I owe it all to you guys. You're such a talented bunch. Being with you all really inspired me and gave me courage," Willow said.

"We inspired each other," Finn replied, slinging his arm around Ella.

"The best part of the nominations has been that we've all gotten to see each other again," Willow said.

"Here, here," Michael agreed, briefly raising his glass, then taking a swig.

"Did Lauren come with you to London?" Ella asked. "She's so lovely. Finn and I always enjoy spending time with her. I know she's eager to travel a bit, so I thought she might accompany you and take a tour of London."

Michael shook his head. "I asked her to come, but Sophie has a dance recital that she didn't want to miss."

"Well, as nice as it would have been to see her, there's something special about the original gang from Sweden being back together," Ella said.

They all got quiet, the air suddenly heavy.

Jean broke the silence. "I can't say I believe in an afterlife, but I'm certain my old friend Albie is still here with us. He damn well would have liked to be at this table, downing a proper bourbon."

Michael laughed, breaking the tension.

"Ella, congratulations on the success of your books. With all the buzz around their release, I felt honored to have been there while you were working on them," Charlotte said.

"Yes, congratulations, *ma chérie*," Jean added.

"Thanks," Ella replied.

"I still can't get the damn sex book out of my mind after all this time," Jean quipped.

Ella giggled.

"We had a great time on her book tour," Finn said, squeezing her shoulder. "Her readings were brilliant. She's so funny, so smart. I was bowled over. There were long lines at each of her signings. Readers can't get enough."

"Finn and I are both road dogs; we loved hopping from city to city. His next film shoots in LA, so it was a nice chance to spread our wings before we head home for a while."

"What's next for you, Ella? Something provocative, no doubt," Charlotte said.

"A philosophical exploration of love."

Jean snorted. "Make sure you write about how romantic love can leave you emotionally and financially bankrupt."

"Ever the optimist," Ella joked as the others laughed.

"I'm just saying, make the book practical. I have one word for you: prenup," Jean said.

"And I have one word for you: fidelity," Ella retorted.

When the group's laughter simmered down, Willow said, "That seems like a hard thing to write a book about, love. It's such a big topic." She looked around nervously. "Is that a stupid thing to say?"

Ella smiled. "Not at all. You're right, which is why I've avoided taking it on until now. Truth be told, I haven't a clue how I'm going to do it. I've been reading, jotting down ideas, hoping somehow it will start to take shape, but I'm still not sure where to start."

"What made you interested in love?" Michael asked.

Ella smiled sweetly at Finn and then looked back at her friends. "Before Finn came along, I was terrified of what happens to our identities when we love. I had always clung to this idea of being whole and autonomous, and that notion seemed counter to what happens to us when *me* becomes *we*." She shook her head and continued, "Like I said, I'm not sure how I'm going to tackle it or where it will lead, only that I'm no longer afraid to find out."

Finn pecked her cheek.

Michael huffed. "I get where you're coming from. If you'd have told me a couple of years ago that I'd be running car pools or spending Saturday nights at home playing board games, I'd have said there wasn't a chance in hell. But now . . ." He paused to take a swig of his drink. "This has been the best time of my life. Lauren is amazing, and Sophie is the greatest kid. I just like hanging out with them."

Willow smiled and Charlotte patted his arm.

"Last time you guys came over to hang out at the pool, Lauren told me what a wonderful father you've become," Ella said.

"Sophie makes it easy. She's so much like her mother: a total sweetheart," Michael replied, a faint smile sweeping across his face.

"There's nothing like being a parent, is there?" Charlotte said.

"Speaking of which, do you have new pictures of your sweet little Rupert?" Ella asked.

"I want to see too!" Willow chimed in enthusiastically.

Charlotte smiled, scrolled through her phone, and then passed it around the table.

"Aww, he's the cutest little thing ever," Willow gushed.

"He's getting so big," Ella added.

"He's beautiful," Finn said, passing the phone back to her.

"So, Ella, Finn, when are you two going to take the leap and pop out a kid or two?" Michael asked.

Charlotte furrowed her brow. "You can't ask people that."

"They're not random people. It's Finn and Ella," he replied with a shrug. "You had your iconic engagement and perfect wedding, but when can we expect to have some little Forresters scampering about?"

"You have to admit, you two would make the cutest babies ever," Willow remarked.

"Hey, now. You all know my wife scares easily," Finn said with a chuckle.

Everyone laughed, including Ella.

"Come on, you both seem like you'd be great parents. Hell, if I can do it, you sure can. Do you want children?" Michael asked.

"We would love to have a family. As for when, that will be up to Ella. She'll let me know when she's ready. So, until then, back the fuck off," Finn said with a laugh.

Michael raised his glass.

Suddenly, Willow started sniffling.

"Are you okay?" Charlotte asked gently, resting a caring hand on Willow's shoulder.

"Yes, I'm sorry," Willow replied, wiping her eyes. "I didn't mean to bring down the table. It's just that I love it when we all get together. When we were in Sweden, you all became like a family to me in a way. I just really wish Albie were here."

"We all feel that way," Charlotte said. "In a way, he is here. After all, we're here for his big award tomorrow night. So really, he's brought us together again."

"I have an idea. Remember in Sweden when we'd play some of my go-around-the-table games?" Ella asked.

"Yeah, baby," Finn said as the others nodded.

"How about we take turns and each say one thing we remember about Albie? It can be anything, something heartfelt or silly. Let's celebrate what he meant to us all before the whole world is in on it tomorrow night."

"That's a great idea. I'll go first," Willow said. "Albie took me seriously as an actress. He praised my performance and said I had a wonderful career ahead, if I made artistic choices. That was a real turning point for me. His advice and confidence in me changed my life. He also told me not to take shit from anyone, and that's come in handy too."

They burst into laughter.

"That reminds me of a time years ago," Jean said, absent-mindedly running his finger along the rim of his glass. "We were on a shoot in Barcelona. Albie was in the dining room, playing a tune on the piano, as he so often did. I started giving him notes about his performance on set that day, telling him about my plans for reshoots the next day. He stopped playing, looked at me, and said, 'I'm off the clock. Grab a drink or bugger off.' Then he went right back to playing," Jean said.

Michael laughed so hard, he spit his drink across the room. "Okay, guess it's my turn. I remember one night in Sweden, when everyone else had gone up to bed, Albie and I stayed for one last drink. One turned into a few. Let's just say, that old geezer drank me under the table. It was embarrassing."

When the group settled down, Charlotte said, "I hate to spoil the fun, but I had so many tender moments with Albie over the years. He was a mentor to me. The first play we did together, God, I was standing in the wings on opening night, shaking like a leaf. He came over, patted my hand, and looked into my eyes with such reassurance. He handed me a penny and said, 'Lucky penny. I always keep one of these in my pocket. If I get nervous on stage, I rub it. Calms me right down. I know a talented woman like you doesn't need those tricks, but take it so I won't feel so alone.'" She stopped to take a breath as her eyes welled up. "To this day, whenever I'm on set, I keep a penny in my pocket."

Finn nodded knowingly. "He was such a generous actor. He gave you so much to work with and so much encouragement to really push yourself. He knew how honored I felt acting alongside him—it was the highlight of my career. After one of our big scenes, we were walking back to our trailers and he said, 'I could hardly keep up with you.' In truth, it had been the other way around, but he was being kind." He turned to Ella and asked, "What about you, sweetheart? What's your fondest memory?"

"I have so many, it's impossible to choose. But I'll never forget when we all celebrated his last birthday, watching him savor each bite of that blueberry tart and the look on his face when he told us how he fell for Margaret. Such a romantic for a crusty old bird." They laughed and she continued, "He told me many times that love is all that matters. 'Love, Ella. Love.' I'll never forget those words."

Finn rubbed her arm, and she smiled at him.

Jean raised his glass. "To Albie, for teaching us all a little something about love."

"To Albie!"

FINN AND ELLA STROLLED DOWN THE long red carpet at the famed Royal Albert Hall, arm in arm behind the rest of the *Celebration* team.

"Somehow I've never been here before," Finn said.

"Well, you're in for a treat. It's extraordinary inside. Concerts here are wonderful."

"I'll have to get us tickets sometime."

"Funny story about how this place came to be. Prince Albert wanted to create a hall to celebrate the arts and sciences, to bring culture to the people. He died before it was completed, and Queen Victoria insisted it should be named after him. They even wove the letter *A* into the stairway railings. Then of course she had that obscenely pricey gold memorial statue created outside, across the road from the hall. She spent the rest of her life wearing black, to show her deep mourning."

"She must have really loved him."

Ella shrugged.

"What?" Finn asked.

"Oh, I don't know. I'm sure she did love him, in her own way, but perhaps it would have meant more to simply realize his vision. He wanted this place to be about the arts, not about him. Love isn't about gold statues or opulence. The grandest gesture is seeing someone for who they are and honoring what's important to them."

He pecked her cheek just as they reached the doorway, where an usher was waiting to escort them to their front row seats. Margaret Hughes, dressed in a black satin gown, her gray hair styled in waves like the night she met Albie, sat between Jean and Ella.

When it was time for the Lifetime Achievement Award, the host called Jean to the stage to present the winner. Ella took Margaret's hand, and they smiled at one another. Jean stood at the podium and said, "Thank you to the British Academy of Film and Television Arts for bestowing this high honor upon my dear friend, the great Albie Hughes. So often, you get these awards wrong, but this time there has been no error." He paused as the audience laughed. "Albie was a gifted actor of stage and screen, one of the greatest I've ever known. He was also a hell of a lot of fun. Truth be told, I cast him in so many roles because I had so much damn fun sharing a bourbon with him after a day of shooting and listening to him tickle the ivories whenever a piano was in the room. Albie was a straight shooter; there was no veneer. He lived life to the fullest, making the most of each experience, and that is what comes through in his many memorable performances."

Jean stepped aside as the lights dimmed and a film highlighting Albie's career played on massive screens, ending with a scene from *Celebration* and still shots of the cast taking their final bow. When the lights came back on, Jean said, "It is with great pleasure that I welcome Margaret Hughes to the stage to accept this award on her husband's behalf."

The entire audience rose. Ella hugged Margaret, and then Finn escorted her up to the stage before returning to his seat. Margaret stood, tears in her eyes and a warm smile on her face as the audience remained on their feet, clapping thunderously. When she caught her breath, she said, "Thank you very much." The audience took their seats. "My darling Albie didn't care much for awards, called them rubbish. It's probably best you waited until he passed to bestow this great honor upon him, else I fear he may not have showed up to accept it and deprived us all of this opportunity." She paused as everyone laughed. "I'd like to thank the Academy for recognizing my husband's body of work, and Jean for that lovely introduction. Albie knew he was ill when he went off to make his last picture. He viewed Jean knocking on his door at that moment as a gift from the universe, a final chance to make a piece of art that would outlast him, or any of us. As it turned out, he became very close to everyone on set and said it was the best shoot of his life. What a glorious way to go out. For that, I'd like to thank the cast and crew of *Celebration*, and all those who were part of that special experience. He was especially grateful to be part of a film that asked life's big questions. Yet for my Albie, the answer was always simple: love. Jean was kind to call him a straight shooter, but the truth is my darling could be a bit of a grump." Everyone laughed and Margaret continued, "But he never failed to believe in love above all else. That's what he brought to his many beloved characters, and it's certainly what he brought to my life. Thank you kindly for this honor."

The audience leaped to their feet in applause. Finn put his arm around Ella and kissed the side of her head as they joined the chorus of cheers.

CHAPTER 10

Finn struggled to clasp his cuff links as Ella emerged from the bathroom in a strapless chartreuse gown that hugged the curves of her body, her long spiral curls pulled into a messy bun, her lips stained red, and strands of sparkles dangling from her ears. "Wow!" Finn exclaimed, his eyes nearly popping out of his head. "You are breathtaking. God, look at your incredible green eyes. I'm . . . I'm speechless."

Ella blushed. "Here, love, let me do that," she said as she fastened his cuff links and smoothed his lapels. "Now you look Oscar worthy. You're impossibly sexy in a tuxedo. Makes me a bit blue that this is our last hurrah."

Finn was barely listening, too fixated on his bride. "I'm serious. You are stunning. Showstopping. I wish we could just stay home," he said, taking a whiff of her perfume. "Are these diamonds?" he asked, touching her earlobe.

"They're costume, paste, I think. Found them at a flea market. The dress is vintage too. Jason helped me scour all the best places until we found the right pieces. I wanted to wear something special and one of a kind for your big night."

"Sweetheart, try not to get your hopes up. I don't have a shot in hell of winning. The whole season, they've been honoring the acting in the film through Willow. It'll be amazing if she wins Best Supporting Actress tonight, such a comeback story. I'm thrilled for her. As for lead actor, Grey Hewson took the Globe and the SAG for that biopic he did. It's his year. I have no expectations of an upset."

"Oh, I don't know. Someone once told me that lightning always strikes when we least expect it. Shortly after, I met you."

"This film already gave me everything I could possibly want," he said, kissing the tip of her nose. "Besides, if there is somehow a surprise tonight, it should be Albie who takes it, posthumously. I'm flattered to be nominated alongside him."

"Trust me, if Albie has any pull from the beyond, he's using it on your behalf. No matter. It's just wonderful how the film has been recognized."

"I've never cared about awards season or any of this stuff, but it's been different this time around. I'm feeling a bit nostalgic. Tonight is the end. It's been a blast reconnecting with Jean and the whole gang, celebrating the film. It reminds me of how our love story began," he said, kissing her forehead.

Ella smiled. "Our love story has many chapters. Maybe after tonight, we'll start writing the next one. But for now, we should party with the gang into the wee hours. Now come on, let's go get you that trophy."

Finn laughed, linking his arm with hers, and they headed out.

"YOU LOOKED SO GORGEOUS ON THE red carpet that I could hardly focus on what the reporters were asking me," Finn whispered as they walked down the theater aisle to their assigned, front row seats. "You'll be on the cover of every magazine tomorrow, yet again. You outshone every actress here."

Ella giggled. "I think you may be biased."

"It wasn't just me; no one could take their eyes off you. Jean practically drooled when we bumped into him. He's still got a crush on you, you know."

"Jealous?" she joked.

"Always."

"Silly. You are my one and only. I'm so lucky to be on the arm of the most handsome, most extraordinary man here, the man of my dreams." They gazed at each other for a moment before she continued, "Did you see Willow speaking with the press? She looks like a fairy princess in that gorgeous, sparkling ball gown. I'm so happy for her."

"If she scores gold tonight, it'll be another one for Albie. He predicted great things for her, and it seems he was always right."

Ella smiled just as Michael and Lauren, as well as Charlotte and her husband, stopped by to say hello on the way to their seats. Ella leaned over and kissed Finn's cheek. "Good luck tonight, my love," she whispered, just as the host took to the stage to begin the ceremony.

Before long, it was time for the final acting category. Out of the corner of her eye, Ella saw Willow clutching her gold statuette, still teary-eyed from her speech in which she dedicated the award to her mother and grandmother. Ella took Finn's hand and gave it a squeeze as the nominees for Best Actor were announced. "And the winner is . . ." The presenter tore the envelope open, did a double take, and announced, "Finn Forrester for *Celebration*!" Finn gasped as the entire audience rose to their feet in a standing ovation. Stunned, he turned to his beaming bride.

"Congratulations, my love," she said, touching his cheek and kissing him softly. He shook his head as if to process what was happening, and then made his way to the microphone as the audience continued to roar.

When everyone finally took their seats, he said, "I am truly floored. Thank you to the Academy for this most incredible, unexpected honor. I have to thank my parents for taking my childhood dream seriously and helping me achieve it." He ran his hand through his hair and shook his head, clearly in shock. "Making this film was the artistic and personal experience of a lifetime. I'm indebted to Jean, the entire crew, and our incredible cast: Charlotte, Michael, Willow, and the incomparable Albie Hughes." He paused to catch his breath as the audience jumped to their feet, cheering. "There's another very special person to whom I owe a great debt, my brilliant wife, Ella, who was on location inspiring us every step of the way." The entire *Celebration* gang turned toward Ella and clapped vigorously. Finn looked directly at his beloved, who had tears in her eyes, and said, "Ella, this will always be the most magical shoot of my life because it's where we met and fell in love. When I look at you, I'm certain that love is everything. Thank you for taking the leap with me and turning my life into this glorious adventure. I'm looking forward to every moment of our journey together, my partner and one true love."

Ella smiled through the tears cascading down her face as Finn held up his award and said, "Thank you so much," before exiting the stage to more applause.

THEY SPENT HOURS CELEBRATING WITH their friends at the after-party, finally wandering into their bedroom at two in the morning, equally exhausted and energized.

Finn set his Oscar down gently on his nightstand. "I still can't believe this happened."

"I believe it and I'm so proud of you," Ella said, brushing her hand along his wrist.

"Tonight was such an incredible way to end the journey of this film, beyond my wildest dreams. It's hard to believe it's over."

"Finn, maybe it's time to start writing the next part of our story."

"What do you mean, love?" he asked.

"I'm ready. Let's make a baby."

He smiled so wide he could hardly speak. "Just when I thought tonight couldn't possibly get better."

"You know, if we're going to try for a baby, we'll need to make love over and over again."

"There's no time like the present. Let me help you out of that gown."

 **CHAPTER 11**

"I love our nightly ritual," Ella said, turning to Finn and running her hand down his arm. "I always read while you review scripts, making your little chicken scratch notations. Without fail, I end up putting my book down and just staring at you—the sexy little lines around your eyes when you concentrate, the shape of your lips when you lean your pen there." She shook her head. "It's silly, but it's been my favorite part of the day since we started our love affair."

He smiled and flung the manuscript onto his nightstand. "That's sweet, baby."

"Your film wraps soon. You must be inundated with offers after your big Oscar win. Have you selected a script for your next project?"

"Yeah. I was just rereading it, actually. It's a high-action blockbuster. It's by no means great or important art, but the script is a lot of fun, much better than most in the genre. They're offering an astronomical payday. I'm not getting any younger. My days as a hero-lead are numbered, so it's time to cash in for our family's future security. It films in LA too, and I figured, if you get pregnant . . ." She smiled and he continued, "Anyway, I told my agent I'd do it, but that he should focus on interesting or challenging indie roles moving forward."

"Sounds like a good plan. And for the record, you'll always be my heroic leading man."

He blushed. "Will you read the script and tell me what you think?"

"Don't I always?" She gave him a little kiss. "I love how we share our passions."

"Me too."

"Maybe that's why I cherish our evenings so much. Plus, it's so cozy in bed with you."

Finn smiled devilishly. "I have to confess that my favorite part of the day is what usually happens next," he said, playfully running his hand along the curves of her body. "Although since we've been trying to conceive, we're doing it morning, noon, and night."

Ella giggled. "Just an added benefit of trying to have a baby—I get to have you any time I want you."

"Speaking of which," he said, dimming the light and pulling her into his arms.

ELLA WAS HUDDLED IN BED, ANXIOUSLY playing with her hair, the script beside her, when Finn finally came home the next evening.

"Hi, sweetheart," he said, leaning down to give her a smooch. "Sorry I'm so late. We had to reshoot a scene about a million times. Mercifully, it's the weekend. I could sure use the time off."

"Uh-huh," she grumbled.

"Did I wake you?" he asked.

"No, I was waiting for you," she replied, propping pillows behind her and sitting up.

"Let me brush my teeth and wash up," he said, darting off to the bathroom. He returned a few minutes later in boxer shorts and slipped into bed beside her. "Hi, baby," he said softly, kissing her. "This is a pretty nightgown."

"Finn, we need to talk," she said, pulling away from him. He looked at her curiously, and she gestured at the script.

"Did you get a chance to read it? What do you think?" he asked.

"I can't believe you would agree to do this. You're married. Didn't you think of that at all? Didn't you think about how this would make me feel?"

"What are you talking about?" he asked, looking bewildered.

"All the sex and kissing," she said quietly, as if she were embarrassed to say it out loud.

"Ella . . ." he muttered, nearly breaking out into laughter. "You can't be serious."

"Don't do that. Don't act like it's nothing. How do you think that makes me feel? The opening scene is you having steamy sex with another woman. Touching another woman's naked body, her touching you, kissing passionately. My God, she's riding you with her bare breasts in your face!"

"It's acting. There's nothing the least bit sexy or romantic about it. You know how movies are filmed and what it's really like."

"What I know is that you and another woman will be more or less naked, touching each other, and kissing. *Kissing*, Finn."

"It doesn't mean anything," he said dismissively.

"It does to me."

"Sweetheart, you're the only woman in the world that I want. You're my one true love. Always. It's just work."

"But I'm telling you it hurts me."

"Ella, I'm an actor. This isn't new. Hell, we met on a film set," he said with exasperation.

She sprang out of bed. "Yeah, and I told you back then that I wouldn't be comfortable watching you be intimate with another woman, acting or not. You said you were glad I felt that way, that's how it should be with people who love each other, and now . . ."

"What?"

"Now you agreed to do this without even considering my feelings."

"Baby," he said, getting out of bed and taking her hands, "please don't turn this into something that it's not. It's a meaningless action movie with the meaningless proverbial eye candy sex scenes."

"Exactly. That's what hurts even more. It's not like this is some great piece of cinematic art and the intimacy is integral to telling the story. You're willing to hurt me for some stupid blockbuster you don't even care about, for money. That's so much worse," she said.

"Please, baby," Finn said, putting his arms around her. Ella held on to him as he rubbed her head. "The first time we kissed, I felt it in every part of my body. I still do, each time. A scripted kissing scene with an actress can't touch what we have. Nothing can. Don't give it another thought."

She pulled back and looked deeply into his eyes. "How can you say that?" She gently ran her finger across his upper lip, following the curve, lingering on the soft raised spot in the center. "This is my favorite part of you," she said, and she lightly pressed her mouth to his. "How could you ever put this part of yourself on someone else? You're breaking my heart, Finn."

"Ella, please. I'm an actor. That doesn't change just because we're married."

"I thought everything changed when we got married. We promised to always put our relationship first."

"Actors have love scenes all the time, and their partners understand. I never thought this would be an issue for you of all people. You're usually so cool." He shook his head like he was annoyed. "Let's table this for now. I'm exhausted and you're being . . ."

"What?" she asked defensively.

"You're being totally unreasonable!" he snapped. "This is absurd. I'm a fucking actor. Get over it!"

She burst into tears and threw her face in her hands.

"Ella," he said gently. He caressed her arms and said, "I'm sorry I shouted. I'm just tired."

She looked at him through a film of tears. "You hurt me, Finn. You promised never to hurt me, and now you have done it without a single thought. What's worst of all is you're trying to make me feel crazy for it."

"This seems so unlike you. Why are you being so emotional?"

"I don't know. I just am. I would hope you'd be emotional if I wanted to kiss another man." She slipped on her silk robe and shuffled to the bedroom door, tears streaming down her face.

"Ella . . ." he called.

"I'm going to sleep in one of the guest rooms. Please just leave me alone. You don't care about how I feel, and it hurts too much to be near you right now," she said, closing the door behind her.

"Fuck," Finn grumbled, pacing around the room and muttering to himself in frustration. "She's being totally irrational. I'm a fucking actor." He sat down on the love seat and gripped his head in his hands. Soon, his mind drifted to the summer he left for Sweden and how his old girlfriend had given him permission to fool around while he was away, how little she cared and how wrong that was, and how right it felt when he fell in love with Ella. Every promise he had ever made to her echoed in his mind as he remembered how her touch made him feel.

Swept away in a swirl of memories, he went to find her, ambling into the nearest guest bedroom. He found her there, lying on her side, her wild spiral curls fanned out behind her, tissues strewn everywhere. Finn lay down, slipped his arm over her, and pressed himself closely to her, the silk of her robe soft on his body. "I'm so sorry, sweetheart," he whispered.

"I never wanted to love you, but you pushed me and now I can't help but to love you. You promised my heart was safe with you," she whimpered.

"It is. I love you so much."

"Have you any idea what it's like?" Ella asked through a sniffle. "I have to see things you never would. There are thousands of photographs of you with every woman you've ever dated, and the media constantly finds ways to splash them all over the place. Your fans have social media accounts dedicated to how hot you are. Some even post about how they can't wait for us to split up so you'll be on the market again."

"Baby, I had no idea. I never look at that junk."

"I try to avoid it, but sometimes it's impossible. It's not always easy to love someone the whole world fantasizes about. Then there are your movies. All those intimate acts recorded forever, images I can't unsee. At least it was all before me, so I have an easier time putting it out of my mind, remembering that it's your job, and focusing on us. But now you want to put more of it into the world. So much of this you can't control, but this . . ." She paused as her voice cracked. "This, you're choosing. You're choosing to kiss someone else."

He sighed. "You're right. You're my partner in every-thing, and I should have taken your feelings into account. I'm so sorry." She sniffled and turned to face him. He wiped the tears from her cheeks. "I've been acting since I was a kid. I've never had to consider anyone else when selecting projects, so it didn't even occur to me. It should have. I'm sorry. You are the most important thing in my world, and I would never want to hurt you. I promise I'll fix this."

She leaned her cheek against his chest, and he cradled her head in his arms. "Maybe I love you too much," she whispered. "I don't know how to love you less."

He dropped a kiss in her hair. "My beautiful Ella. Don't ever love me less."

ELLA OPENED HER EYES AT THE EARLY morning light, still nestled against Finn. "Hey, you," he said, kissing the top of her head.

"You're up early."

"I barely slept. Baby, I'm so sorry about the movie. You were right. The more I think about it and how I would feel if things were reversed, I know it's not worth it. I'm going to call my agent. Nothing's been signed, so it's not too late to get out of it."

"Finn, that isn't what I want."

"I don't understand. I thought . . ."

"What I want is for you to take my feelings seriously. I want to be a factor in your decision-making."

"But you said the sex scenes are too much for you, that if I have to kiss an actress it will break your heart."

"It will. A little piece of it. So, when you're choosing which roles to take, I hope you'll think about that, think about what's being asked of you and how it will make me feel. Think about how our children may feel one day if they see it. Then weigh all of it up against the quality of the script, how badly you want the part, how important the sexy stuff is to the film. Finn, I know you're an actor—a beautiful, gifted performer," she said, sweeping her fingertips down his face. "I know that's a big part of who you are, and I don't want to control it or take it away from you. But we have linked our lives. It's not just you anymore. What you do affects me. It can change things between us. I'm just asking you to remember that. Prioritize our relationship along with whatever else you want for yourself. I love you. Please be gentle with my heart." She paused to consider her words. "This is new for both of us. I don't know what all the answers are, but there must be a way to balance who we each are with who we are together."

Finn kissed her forehead. "I'll make it my mission to find that balance. As for this movie, after thinking about what you said last night, I don't know if I could ever kiss someone else again, even though it's only work. I certainly couldn't manage to make it look believable. What we have is so special, and I don't want to do anything to diminish or change it. Hurting you is unbearable."

"Give it some time. Mull it over. I love you for who you are, and you're an artist. I knew the score from day one. The last thing I'd ever want is for you to feel you have to choose between me and something you want for yourself. All I'm asking is that you consider me. Consider us."

"I promise I will. I hope you know what you mean to me."

"Well . . . how about you show me in a private love scene?" Ella suggested, pulling him closer.

A WEEK LATER, FINN CALLED ELLA from his trailer during some downtime on set.

"Hey, you," she answered.

"Hi, sweetheart. My agent just got back to me. He told them I wouldn't do it without specific rewrites to the script. They hemmed and hawed for a few days, but in the end, they were fine with it. They wanted my name attached for the box office appeal."

"No surprise there. You are the best," she said.

"The opening scene has been changed. There's a naked woman in my character's bed, but he just gets out of bed and walks to the bathroom. The sex is implied. I never even touch her. Most importantly, no kissing. They actually like it better this way—fits the unattached, tough-guy nature of the character."

She giggled. "I'm glad it worked out. It would seem that art and life can sometimes harmoniously coexist. Thank you for doing this for me."

"This is what I should have done in the first place. It's for us and it's exactly how it should be."

"I love you. Funny timing, you calling. I was just think-ing about you."

"Oh yeah?" Finn said. "What were you thinking?"

"Something I can't say over the phone. I was actually about to call you. Any chance you'll be able to get home for dinner tonight? I was hoping for a romantic night with my husband, and it can't wait. I'll make something special."

"If we stay on schedule, I should be able to get out of here by seven, eight at the latest. Can we do dinner on the later side?"

"Yes. I'll be waiting for you."

"ELLA, I'M HOME," FINN CALLED.

"In here," she replied.

He walked into the dimly lit dining room to find a beau-tifully set table covered with glowing candles, rose petals, and two plates beneath silver cloches. Ella was standing in a sheer white dress, her long spirals flowing freely, and the green amber necklace that Finn had bought her in Sweden dangling from her neck. "Wow! You are stunning. I'm sorry I'm late. I got here as soon as I could," he said, giving her a peck.

"You're worth the wait."

He blushed and kissed her again. "I hope dinner isn't spoiled."

"Everything is perfect. I made salmon in a caviar sauce. Do you remember?"

He nodded. "That's what I had prepared for us that night in Sweden."

"That was the first time we shared our dreams for the future. You said there was no fantasy we couldn't make a reality as long as we were together."

"I still believe that. More than ever."

"Me too," she said. "Before dinner, will you dance with me?"

"I would love to."

She turned on the music, and Elvis Presley's "Can't Help Falling in Love" floated into the room. "Our wedding song," he said, taking her hand. They swayed with their bodies pressed closely together, staring deeply into each other's eyes, their faces practically touching. When the song ended, Ella's eyes filled with tears.

"What is it, my love?" he whispered.

She smiled through her tears. "We're having a baby, Finn. I'm pregnant."

"Oh my God," he mumbled. He smiled brightly, took her face in his hands, and gently pressed his mouth to hers. "That's the best news I've ever heard. I love you so much, Ella. With all my heart."

AFTER A SUCCULENT DINNER, DURING which they were too giddy to even speak, they wandered into their bedroom hand in hand. Finn touched her cheek. "You look so beautiful, so radiant. It must be true that pregnant women glow."

Ella smiled, turned around, and lifted her hair away from her neck. "Will you take my necklace off?"

He unfastened the chain and placed it on her vanity. He blew on the nape of her neck, and she let her hair down and turned toward him. Without a word, he gingerly pulled her dress over her head and then dropped down to his knees, slipping her underwear off and putting his mouth on her until she squealed. "I need you," she said, pulling him up. She quickly unbuttoned his shirt and helped him out of the rest of his clothes. He picked her up and carefully laid her on the bed, gazing deeply into her eyes, stroking the side of her face, and kissing her intimately.

After making love, Finn caressed Ella's shoulder, unable to peel his eyes off her. Eventually, in a faint voice, he said, "I love you so much I don't even have the words for it. You make me happier than I ever thought was possible."

"I feel the same way about you. That was so beautiful. Something was different between us."

"I've never wanted to be so gentle with someone. I was so lost in you." He shook his head. "I can't explain it, the way I feel about you. It's so deep. All-encompassing."

She pecked his lips. "We made a baby."

He smiled. "How did you know?"

"My period was late, and I've been feeling so emotional and out of sorts lately. It suddenly occurred to me that maybe we'd gotten lucky. I thought it was too soon since we only started trying a couple of months ago, but . . ."

"We were made to make babies together."

She rubbed the tip of her nose to his. "When I took the pregnancy test, and later when the doctor confirmed it, this profound, peaceful joy bubbled up inside of me. It was torture keeping the news to myself. I couldn't wait to tell you."

"You didn't have to go by yourself. I promised you that if we had children, you wouldn't go to so much as a single doctor's appointment alone. I'll do everything with you. I want us to go through this pregnancy together, and when our baby is born, I want to be a hands-on parent. I'll do everything in my power to be the best father I can possibly be."

"I know, and I love you for it. Our baby is so lucky to have you."

He rested his hand on her tummy. "I already love them more than I can say. Ella, you are my world. The family we're creating is my world. Please know you'll always come first."

She kissed him softly. "Finn, I want us to raise our family together, just you and me. No nannies or anything like that. We already have people cooking our food and doing our laundry. I want us to be the ones taking care of our children—guiding them, enjoying them."

"I want that too." He chuckled and asked, "But we can hire a babysitter from time to time, right?"

"Yes, of course," she replied through a smile. "I know we're both passionate about our work, but . . ."

"We'll figure it out. We'll make it work. Our way. As partners."

"Can I tell you something?" Ella asked.

"Anything."

"You know I've never been much of a planner, and I don't dwell on the future, but after I found out I'm pregnant, I thought about holding our newborn, watching them grow up, and before long, I was daydreaming about being old with you, about how handsome you'll look with gray hair and deep lines on your face," she said, tracing the soft lines around his eyes. "I imagined our adult children and lots of sweet little grandchildren running around. At the center of it all was the two of us, together, enjoying them all, as in love as the day we got married. Maybe it's silly, but I can see it so clearly."

Finn smiled and kissed her forehead. "It's not silly to me. I see it too, just as you described. Like I've always said: with how we feel about each other, there's no fantasy we can't make a reality. I'm so excited for this next part of our adventure."

"Me too. We're having a baby," she whispered, tears in her eyes.

"We're having a baby."

 **CHAPTER 12**

"Finn, I need you," Ella said, grabbing his bicep to pull him closer. She guided his hand between her legs. "Oh, yes," she moaned with delight.

"That's it, baby, that's it. Come here," he said, sitting up and pulling her into his lap. He swept her hair back and started kissing her ear, neck, and mouth.

"I'm so in love with you," she whispered.

"Oh my God," Finn groaned as he held Ella's hips and thrust against her until they both let out sounds of bliss. They held each other tightly, trying to catch their breath. "Lie down with me," he whispered.

Finn caressed her arm and planted a soft kiss on her mouth. "I can't believe how many times we make love each day."

"There's nothing else I want to do," she said.

"These pregnancy hormones are incredible!"

"Every time you even brush past me, I just have to have you. You are the sexiest man I've ever seen, and you're all mine."

He blushed. "This is the most erotic time in my life. I've never been so attracted to someone in my life, or so in love."

"The magnetic pull between us is so strong. I wondered what it would be like, my body changing, but I've never felt better, more alive, or closer to you. Or this sensual," she said, running her finger down his face.

"You just get more and more beautiful by the day. I love this sweet little baby bump that's starting to pop," he said, rubbing her tummy.

She smiled. "At our appointment this afternoon, they'll do an ultrasound. We need to decide whether we want to know the sex. It's a little early, but sometimes they can tell by now."

"It's up to you, sweetheart. I'll follow your lead."

"I never thought I'd be someone who would want to know. True surprises are so rare in life," she said.

"Some people find out so they can design the nursery, but you've never been a planner, and I sure as hell can't imagine we're going the traditional pink or blue route."

Ella giggled. "That's for sure. It's just . . ."

"What, sweetheart? Do you want to find out?"

"I feel so close to you and to our baby, closer than I ever thought I could be to anyone. We're connected in a way that's impossible to explain."

"I know. I feel it too," Finn said, leaning his forehead against hers.

"It would be nice if our baby had a name. Bonding, you know?"

"Then let's find out," he said with a smile.

She kissed him lightly.

"The first time we spoke about having a family, soaking in that bubble bath, you said you fantasized that we'd have three children. Two girls, and then a boy. Do you still picture it that way?" he asked.

"Yes, but it doesn't matter. All that matters is that we're doing it together."

"If we had a daughter, we said we'd call her Betty. We never came up with a name for a boy."

"I have an idea I think you'll like," Ella said, "but let's wait until we need a name."

"Okay."

"You know what can't wait, though?"

"What's that?"

"Me. I need you right now, so I hope you're ready for the next round," she said, wrapping her arms around his neck and kissing him passionately.

"MRS. FORRESTER, I AM A LITTLE concerned about your weight. By the eighteenth week, I would have expected you to have gained a little more than you have. Usually, we see a two-to-four-pound weight gain in the first twelve weeks, and then a pound or two each week after, so you're below the typical benchmark. Have you been eating the recommended daily calories we discussed?" Dr. King asked.

"Yes," Ella replied, looking alarmed. "I've never eaten so much in my life! I've made a point of it. I'm exercising, running and doing yoga, which you said was safe since I was already athletic, but I'm not overdoing it. I don't know why . . ."

"Relax," Dr. King said, smiling warmly. "You have an ultra-lean body type to begin with, and some women don't really start to gain weight until later in pregnancy. You may be one of those lucky women who naturally carries small. Let's just keep an eye on it."

"All right," Ella replied. "I just started to feel the baby move a few days ago. Little flutters, like a butterfly whizzing around. Finn can't feel it yet. Is that normal?"

"Yes, perfectly normal. It will probably be a few more weeks until the baby is large enough and their kicks are strong enough for someone touching your belly to feel it. Now, would you two like to see your child?" she asked.

"We can't wait," Finn said with a grin.

"Please lie back and lift your gown. I'm going to rub this jelly on your tummy. Sorry if it's a little cold."

Finn held Ella's hand, and they smiled at each other with joyful anticipation.

"Okay, I need to push down to get a clear image, so this could be a bit uncomfortable. Ah, there's your baby."

"Oh my God," Finn muttered. He looked at Ella, and their eyes welled up.

"That's our baby," Ella mumbled, smiling through her tears.

"Let's listen to the heartbeat," Dr. King said as a beautiful thumping noise filled the room.

Finn leaned down and kissed Ella's forehead.

"Would you like to know the sex? Your baby isn't shy and I have a clear view."

"Yes, please," Ella replied.

"Congratulations, Mom and Dad!" Dr. King said. "It's a girl!"

"Betty!" Finn and Ella both exclaimed as tears slid down their cheeks.

FIVE WEEKS LATER, ELLA WAS working in her office when Finn knocked on the door and let himself in. "I'm sorry to interrupt. How are my girls?"

"Happy to see you. Isn't that right, Betty?" she said, patting her stomach. "How did filming go today?"

"Fine. They took forever setting up the shot, so I spent most of the day hanging out in my trailer and reading baby books. We're still on schedule to wrap in four weeks."

"Good. Then we'll work on the nursery. Lorraine and I have so many ideas, and we can enjoy some time alone before our little one arrives."

"I just wanted to let you know that dinner is ready. Joyce said she can keep things warm if you like. There's no rush."

"Heavens, I completely lost track of time," Ella said, noticing it had gotten dark out.

"Making progress on your book?" he asked.

She nodded. "Still just notes, but I've been writing about the triad of love between partners and their children. It's so abstract, yet material in ways I'd never understood before. Every idea leads to a new question. For instance, when we love so deeply, where do we end and where does the other begin? That's going to be the centerpiece of the book."

"And what do you think the answer is?"

She shrugged. "Stay tuned."

He laughed and said, "Well, let me know when you figure it out."

"You'll be the first to know. I should warn you, I have a new section called 'Erotic Motherhood.' It may be a bit risqué. You know how I can be, pushing the bounds and all. Let's just say, you inspired me."

Finn's cheeks turned pink as he crossed the room to her, leaning down to give her a passionate kiss. "I don't want to disturb you. Find me when you're ready for dinner."

"I'm ready now. I always want to be where you are. Besides, Betty is ravenous," she said, patting her tummy. She closed her laptop and rose. "Oh, Betty," she said with a suddenness.

"Ella, what is it?"

"Our sweet girl is kicking furiously. Feels like acrobatics. Here, feel," she said, placing his hand on her belly.

A huge grin spread across Finn's face. "I can feel her. I . . . I . . ."

She ran her fingers through his hair. "Amazing, isn't she?"

"Yes, she is." He crouched down and spoke to the baby bump. "Your mama and I love you so much, Betty. We've loved you since you were just a dream."

"Oh, did you feel that?" Ella asked. "She's doing cartwheels now."

He smiled and kissed her belly.

"WHAT DO YOU FEEL LIKE THIS MORNING?" Joyce asked.

"Avocado toast with poached eggs, please. Ooh, and I think I'll snack on this while you're making it," Ella replied, retrieving an apple from the fruit bowl. She sat on a barstool, patted her belly, and said, "I'm so hungry in the mornings. Betty just can't wait until breakfast."

"Has she been kicking a lot?" Joyce asked.

Ella nodded. "Ever since she started last week, it's like she can't stop."

Joyce smiled and went to the refrigerator to fetch the eggs and bread.

"I'll grab an avocado," Ella said, rising. "Oh, jeez."

"A big kick?" Joyce asked, turning to look.

"No . . . I . . . I must have stood up too quickly. I feel a bit woozy, and . . ." Before Ella could complete her thought, she fainted. Joyce rushed to break her fall, catching her limp body.

"CUT!" THE DIRECTOR YELLED.

"What the hell was that?" Finn asked his costar. "We were in the middle of a scene."

The director hurried over to Finn and quietly said, "Someone from your house just called. There's an emergency with your wife. She's been taken to the hospital by ambulance."

The color drained from his face as he sprinted off the set without a word.

FINN BURST INTO THE EMERGENCY room and saw Joyce. He ran over, his face flushed. "What happened?"

"We were hanging out in the kitchen, making breakfast. She said she felt dizzy, and then she just fainted. Luckily, I broke her fall," Joyce said, her face lined with worry. "Her doctor met us here. I haven't heard anything yet. She's in room 217, down that hall and on the left."

Finn flew down the corridor and into Ella's room, where she was sitting in bed, eating crackers.

"I'm okay," she said as he raced to her side. "The baby too. They did an ultrasound."

He threw his arms around her, rubbing her head, and she held him tightly. Eventually, he pulled back and took her hand in his. "What did the doctor say?"

"Nothing yet, really. She just did the ultrasound, which was fine, and she said she'd be back in a few minutes. Finn, what if . . . what if something is wrong with the baby, and . . ."

"Shh. There's nothing wrong with Betty. Let's just wait until we know more."

"But what if . . ."

They were interrupted when Dr. King came into the room. "Sorry about the delay," she said. "I was just ordering a few tests for you. I'm glad your husband is here."

"Doctor, what's going on? What would cause my wife to faint?" Finn asked.

"That's what we're going to try to figure out. Ella, have you felt lightheaded before?"

"Yes, every once in a while for the past few weeks, if I get up too quickly or something like that," Ella replied.

Finn looked at her, surprised. "Sweetheart, why didn't you say anything?"

"I thought it was normal. I didn't realize . . . I didn't know . . ."

"Ella," Dr. King interjected, trying to keep them from panicking, "how have you felt otherwise? Any pain, cramps, other discomfort?"

Ella shook her head. "No, nothing like that. I've felt great. Sometimes I get a little tired or I feel like my energy is a bit low, but that's all."

"What about nausea?"

Ella shook her head. "Not at all. Honestly, I've never felt better."

"Nausea can cause some women to avoid eating. You're still well below what we typically see for weight gain. Are you getting the recommended daily caloric intake we discussed?"

"Yes," Ella replied.

"Are you sure you're getting proper nutrition?" Dr. King asked. "If you're undereating, it would explain these bouts of lightheadedness and low energy."

"That's not it. There must be something else, something really wrong," Ella said, fear etched all over her face.

"We'll get to the bottom of this. I know it's difficult, but please try not to worry. The ultrasound was totally normal; her heartbeat is strong. A nurse will come by in a few minutes to take you to the lab for some blood work. I'll check on you afterward, and if you're feeling better, we'll spring you from this place."

"All right," Ella said.

As soon as the doctor left, Finn took a deep breath and left a lingering kiss on Ella's forehead. "Sweetheart, you know I think you're the most beautiful woman in the world, and I love your pregnant body," he said, placing a hand on her belly. "I'm so attracted to you and I always will be. Nothing is more important than your health and Betty's health. It's natural to gain weight, and . . ."

"What are you saying?" she snapped.

"Just that you've always been so thin and toned. I can understand if maybe you're a little anxious about your body changing. But you don't need to be, and—"

"You think I'm not eating enough? That I'm purposefully undereating because of some vain beauty standard?"

"I don't think you're vain at all, just that maybe you're concerned about . . ."

"You don't trust me," Ella said, shaking her head in hurt and anger. "How could you think I would put anything above our baby's health? You're not listening to me. The doctor isn't listening to me," she said as her eyes filled with tears. "I've been eating just like I'm supposed to be. It has to be something else. There might be something wrong with the baby, and . . ."

"Ella . . ."

Just then, a nurse came in. "I'm ready to take you to the lab for your blood work, Mrs. Forrester."

"I'll go with you," Finn said.

"Stay here," Ella insisted, looking away from him.

He sighed, kissed her forehead, and said, "I'm sorry I upset you."

The nurse helped her into a wheelchair and they left. Finn wandered out to the waiting area and found Joyce, who was wringing her hands with worry. She jumped up and asked, "How are Ella and the baby?"

"They're both okay. The doctor is running some tests, and then Ella will probably be released." He paused and said, "Joyce, I haven't been home much since filming began. Has Ella been eating well?"

"Yes. She used to just have breakfast and dinner; she'd be too busy with work to stop for lunch, so I would just bring afternoon tea to her office. Ever since she found out she's pregnant, she's been having me make her three meals a day, plus a couple of snacks. Instead of tea, she has a green juice every afternoon for extra folic acid for the baby. She still likes to eat clean—fish, lean meats, and lots of fresh veggies—but she's added more carbs to her diet too, like multigrain toast."

Finn huffed and said, "Thank you."

"I've read up on nutrition during pregnancy. I think I'm well-versed. Did I do something wrong?" Joyce asked.

"No, not at all. I did."

He returned to Ella's room and waited until the nurse brought her back. When they were alone again, he stroked her forehead and said, "I'm so sorry, sweetheart. I was grasping at straws, desperately trying to find an answer, something we could fix. I'm just scared."

"You didn't trust me. Do you know how hurtful that is?" Ella asked. "You broke our pact. We promised that our relationship would always be at the center of our lives."

"I *do* trust you. I'm so sorry. Hurting you is the last thing I ever want to do. Please, Ella, let's just focus on making sure that you and Betty are both well. Let's focus on how much we love each other and how much we love her. Nothing else matters."

She nodded.

Dr. King came into the room and asked, "How are you feeling?"

"Fine."

"All right, I'm going to discharge you. Please take it easy for a day or two. Skip your workouts. If you feel dizzy, lie down. A fall could be dangerous for you and the baby. I've put a rush on the labs, and I'll call you later today with the results. If nothing out of the ordinary turns up, just continue taking your prenatal vitamins and make sure you eat and sleep well. We'll take it from there."

After the doctor left, Finn noticed Ella's morose expression and realized she needed to be cheered up. He kissed her temple and said, "I can't wait to get my girls home so I can spoil you rotten. I'll be at your beck and call."

She smiled dimly.

"How's Betty?" he asked, placing his hand on her belly. "This has been an adventurous day. Has she been kicking up a storm?"

"It kicked a little while ago," she said despondently.

Finn winced, but he tried not to show it.

"Please hand me my clothes," Ella said.

ELLA SHUFFLED INTO THEIR BEDROOM, Finn following closely behind.

"Are you hungry, sweetheart? I can ask Joyce to fix you something."

She shook her head. "It's not because I'm not eating. They gave me a banana and crackers at the hospital, and I'm just . . ."

"I know, baby," he said, embracing her. "Why don't we change into our comfy pajamas and slip into bed. Production of the film is on hold indefinitely so I can stay with you. Family first always. We can spend the next couple of days just lounging around and watching movies. Your choice."

"I'm not an invalid," she protested, still barely meeting his eyes.

"Of course not, but the doctor said you should take it easy."

"She didn't say I need total bed rest."

"Come here," Finn said, guiding her to the edge of the bed. "Please sit." She obliged and he took her hand. "Ella, something inside of me fundamentally changed when I found out you're pregnant. It made me feel fiercely protective of you. It's innate, impossible to explain. Today, when I got that phone call . . ." He stopped to shake his head. "I've never been so scared in all my life. Even if I'm overreacting, please indulge me. Just stay in bed for a day or two. I'll stay with you the whole time. Please, for me."

"Fine," she grumbled. "I need to use the bathroom."

A few minutes later, wearing fleece pajamas, she joined Finn in bed. "I'm tired. I'm going to take a nap," she said, lying down with her back to him.

He cradled his body against hers and draped his arm over her.

Two hours later, Ella woke up, Finn still firmly pressed against her. She turned to face him, and he asked, "How's my beautiful wife feeling?"

"Fine."

"How's our little girl?" he asked, putting his hand on her tummy.

"It's fine," she mumbled.

"Oh, Ella," he said, running his fingertips down her face. "Sweetheart, please talk to me. I know what you're doing."

She furrowed her brow.

"You're not using her name anymore. You're using the most detached language you possibly can. I first noticed it in the hospital, but I'd hoped it was just a slip under the stress. I know you, baby. This is what you do when you're scared. You pull away, retreat into yourself, try to make yourself love less. But we have each other and we always will, so you don't need to do that. Let me help you."

"Finn . . ."

"Don't do this. Not with Betty. Please, baby. Lean on me. I'm here."

Ella burst into tears. Finn pulled her close and she rested her head on his chest, sobbing. "When they were rushing me to the hospital, I thought I might lose her. I'm terrified something is really wrong. The more I love her, the more it will hurt," she sputtered in between sobs.

"Oh, sweetheart," he said, rubbing her head. "I was scared too. For both of you. But in my heart, I know she's okay. The ultrasound confirmed it. What she needs now is our love, our boundless love."

She sniffled and pulled back to look at him. He used his fingers to gently wipe away her tears.

"Ella, my partner, my love. We already learned this lesson. You said that when you tore yourself out of my arms in Sweden, it was the most painful experience of your life. Trying to detach yourself from me didn't ease the pain; it amplified it. When we came back together, we made the decision to love fearlessly, with everything we have. That's what we need to do now."

"Okay. You're right. I'm sorry," she said, more tears falling.

"Shh . . ." he said, wiping her tears and kissing her forehead. "You have nothing to apologize for. I can only imagine how frightening it was. I'm so sorry I wasn't there by your side. And about what happened in the hospital . . ."

"It's okay. You were just responding to what the doctor said."

"It's not okay, and I'm so sorry. I was scared, feeling helpless, desperate to make things better. You're already the most incredible mother—the way you take care of yourself, the way you take care of our sweet girl. I should have trusted you implicitly. Please forgive me."

She kissed him softly. "There's nothing to forgive. I love you."

"I love you with all my heart."

They shared a quiet moment, but the silence was broken when the phone rang. Finn glanced at the incoming number and said, "It's Dr. King."

"Put it on speaker," Ella said, sitting as straight as a board.

"Hello, Dr. King. Ella and I are both on the line."

"We got your blood work back and found our culprit. Ella, you have extremely low iron, which explains the dizzy spells."

"I don't understand. I've been eating—"

"Low iron isn't uncommon. It may have already been an issue for you without causing any noticeable symptoms. Pregnancy can exacerbate it in many women. A fetus is like a parasite, sucking up all the nutrients we take in."

"So I didn't do anything wrong?" Ella asked.

"Not at all," Dr. King replied.

Ella's eyes became watery, and she exhaled slowly. Her posture visibly relaxed. "I'm sorry. We're still here."

"The good news is that this problem is easily remedied. Start taking a daily iron supplement. They're available over the counter. And pack as much iron into your diet as you can."

"Okay, I will. Thank you, Doctor," Ella said.

"Take it easy. Bye."

Finn hung up the phone, and Ella exploded into tears again. He held her in a comforting embrace and said, "Oh, baby. This is great news. It's nothing serious."

"I'm just so happy Betty is okay. She's okay, she's okay."

FINN JUMPED OUT OF BED TO ANSWER a knock on the door as Ella watched the end credits roll. "Jason stopped by with the iron pills, and I've made you lunch," Joyce said, carrying a bed tray, which she placed in front of Ella.

"Thank you. This soup smells delicious," Ella said.

"I thought soup would be soothing on a day like today. It's an iron-rich twist on Italian wedding soup: beef broth with small meatballs, potatoes, and lots of kale for folic acid. There's a side of my homemade quinoa crackers too. Later, if you want something sweet, I've made cookies loaded with healthy ingredients. You can have them with cashew milk, which I read is also high in iron." Joyce turned to Finn and said, "I'll bring a tray up for you too so you can eat together."

"Thank you, Joyce," Finn replied, "for everything."

"Mmm, this is so good," Ella said, slurping a big spoonful. "Sorry, I couldn't wait. Betty's hungry."

Finn chuckled. "So, what do you want to watch next? A thriller? An indie?"

"How about a rom-com? That way we're guaranteed love, laughs, and a happy ending."

"ELLA," FINN SAID QUIETLY, rubbing her hair.

"Hmm?" she mumbled, barely opening her eyes.

"I'm sorry to wake you. I have an early call time and . . ."

"What?" she asked through a yawn.

"I just wanted to make sure you're still okay with me going back to work."

"Uh-huh. I've never felt better. It's amazing how quickly those supplements helped. No dizzy spells the last couple of days, and my energy is way up," she said as another yawn slipped out.

He laughed.

"Well, when I'm allowed to sleep, that is," she said.

"Go back to sleep. Call if you need anything at all. I'll have my phone on, even when we're filming."

"Uh-huh. Have a great day," she said, closing her eyes.

He kissed her forehead. "You too, my love. Be brilliant and take care of our girl."

CHAPTER 13

"**I**'m so sorry about our present," Lauren said, cringing with mortification. "Michael insisted he had the perfect idea. I knew it was bad when he wanted to go to the liquor store."

Ella laughed. "It's great. Who doesn't want booze and cigarettes at their baby shower?"

Lauren smiled sheepishly. "He swore you'd get it. Something about how you all hung out in Sweden when you and Finn met," she said, biting her lip. "I still wish we had gotten you a Diaper Genie. Someone, please give her another present to take the spotlight off the world's most inappropriate baby gift."

"Well, you're gonna love this next one from your mother," Finn said. "Close your eyes."

She obliged while he held up a framed charcoal drawing Carmen had made. "Open your eyes."

"Oh, wow!" Ella exclaimed, looking at her own serene likeness: holding her baby bump in all her pregnant glory. Finn held it up so the guests could see, to a chorus of oohs, aahs, and gasps.

"That's gorgeous. You look blissful. It captures you entirely," Marni remarked. "Did you pose for it?"

Ella shook her head. "It's a complete surprise. About a month ago, Finn convinced me to let him take nude photos of me, tastefully, of course. He said he wanted to remember what I looked like carrying our little girl."

"Pregnancy has been such a special time for us," Finn explained. "Ella's never been more spectacularly beautiful. I could never forget how radiant she is. The truth is, Carmen and I had conspired. She wanted to commemorate her daughter carrying her granddaughter, so I sent her the photos. Since Carmen couldn't be here today, she shipped the final artwork and I had it framed." He turned to Ella and said, "I thought we could hang it in our bedroom."

She nodded.

"Okay, Ella. Open mine next. It'll lighten the mood," Marni said, handing her a hot-pink gift box.

"Well, the heat is off Lauren. You and Michael did not get me the most inappropriate gift of the day," Ella said, removing a large vibrator from the box.

"It's the top-of-the-line model," Marni said matter-of-factly. She looked quite proud of herself.

"This is the strangest baby shower ever," Ella remarked. "First was that cake shaped like a newborn baby. Slicing into the head really didn't feel right; the red jelly oozing out was fucked."

Finn laughed.

Marni rolled her eyes. "I told you I wanted to get the cake shaped like a big dick. It had two cream-filled balls on either side. Finn vetoed it."

"It's a baby shower, not a Vegas bachelorette party," Finn said.

Marni shrugged. "I thought it made sense to celebrate how the baby got here in the first place. If it helps, the cake was very flattering to you."

Ella giggled. "You're a good friend. We share the same

twisted, slightly obscene sense of humor. But a vibrator as a baby shower gift? Really?"

"Actually, it's very practical. I read that orgasms can induce labor. So, if you've had enough and want to get that sucker out of you, I figured that this may be the most expedient way to go," Marni explained.

Everyone laughed.

"Thanks for the thought, but I think Finn has me covered in that department," Ella said.

Finn blushed.

"No doubt," Marni said. "But maybe the poor guy could use a break."

Ella turned to Finn. "What do you think, love? Am I too much to handle now that I'm carrying this little basketball?"

Finn covered his eyes with his hands. "I'm so embarrassed, being that my mother is here and all."

"Don't worry, son. I know how babies are made," Barbara said. "Marni's right about the orgasm thing too. That's how we finally got you out, more than a week past due. We did it on the couch. I was too tired to schlep all the way to the bedroom."

"This just gets worse and worse. Like a ten-car pileup," Finn lamented, his face in his hands. "But for the record, Marni, if Ella needs help in that department, I'm more than capable."

"So I've heard," Marni replied with an exaggerated wink.

"Okay, the next gift, please, before my husband flees the scene," Ella said, giggling.

"You can save Dante's present for later. It's just lube and some accessories—we went shopping together," Marni said.

Ella laughed and shook her head.

"Not exactly the most conventional shower gifts so far," Marni commented, reading the list she had been dutifully recording. "A bottle of bourbon and carton of smokes from

Michael and Lauren, a children's philosophy book from Jade, which your kid can't read until at least high school, a nude portrait from your mother, and a vibrator with all the accoutrements. But then again, you are this generation's most infamous sex and pleasure writer, so what did you expect?"

"Well, we did get some more traditional gifts. Willow sent a princess-themed mobile for the crib, Charlotte sent an engraved silver rattle, and of course Barbara made us that beautiful handsewn baby blanket," Ella said, smiling at her mother-in-law. "I can't wait to see what's in that last box. Something surprising, no doubt."

"Here you go," Marni said, handing it to her.

"Oh, it's from Jean. He sent it from Paris." Ella opened the box and removed an envelope. She read the card aloud: "*Ma chérie*. You know my view of human existence is rather dark. As far as I can see, the human race is doomed and the most we can hope for is a good fuck every once in a while to take the edge off." She paused as everyone laughed. "Witnessing firsthand the love you and Finn share makes me think that perhaps there is more, perhaps all is not lost. Wishing you both great joy with your impending arrival. As for the gift, on each of my shoots, I ask everyone in the cast and crew to sign the title page of my copy of the script. I save them all in my personal archive. Given how you and Finn fell in love on location and what we all meant to each other, I thought you two would like to have this to share with your child." She removed the tissue paper from the box and took out something encased in Bubble Wrap. She tore away the packaging to reveal a framed script from *Celebration*, signed by all their friends. Albie's signature was in the center with a heart-shaped swirl under his name. Ella's eyes flooded.

Finn leaned down and kissed the top of her head. "I never would have figured Jean to be so sentimental. What an amazing gift."

Ella wiped her eyes and said, "We can hang it in Betty's room so, when she's old enough, we can tell her our story, and hers."

"DID YOU ENJOY YOUR SHOWER, SWEETHEART?" Finn asked as they snuggled on the couch with their cat after all the guests had left.

"Very much. I had no idea it was coming either. With the due date less than two weeks away, I just figured no one had planned a shower, which would have been fine."

"Not a chance. Your mother needed time to make her present, and Marni thought you'd be more surprised this way."

"She really likes you, you know, Marni. When we first moved in together, she had her doubts, being a skeptic about relationships and all. She thought you were too good to be true and that I'd turn into something I'm not, lose who I am. But now even she sees that we're made for each other."

"That's because we are," he said, pecking her on the lips. He chuckled. "Even though I decided to host the shower in our home, she insisted on taking care of all the details. I did what I could to steer her toward something respectable, but it was impossible. She's a trip."

"It was perfect. Felt like me, us." She gave him a smooch. "I still argue that the cake was totally fucked."

"That it was," he agreed as they both laughed. "But I would have died if she'd have gone with the dick cake in front of my mother. Oh, she also suggested a cake shaped like two breasts—you know, to celebrate your changing body. Holy shit!"

Ella laughed. "Sounds about right." She got quiet for a moment and rubbed her belly. "Something I ate really didn't agree with me. I've been having indigestion, and it's just getting worse and worse. It was probably that demented cake."

"Baby, how long have you felt that way?"

"About an hour. I didn't want to say anything and spoil the fun. I'm sure I'll feel better soon."

"Maybe I should take you to the hospital to be safe."

"Don't be silly. I'm just going to go take a little nap. Help me up."

Finn stood up and took her hands. As she rose, she doubled over. "Oh, jeez. It really is getting worse. You don't think this could be labor, do you?"

"Sweetheart, let's go to the hospital, just in case."

"All right," Ella conceded. "Maybe that's not such a bad idea."

"I'll grab your suitcase and call Dr. King on the way."

"YOU'RE TWO CENTIMETERS DILATED," Dr. King said, peeking up from between Ella's legs. "This could be a long haul, but I'd like to admit you for now. The nurse will continue to monitor you."

"Thank you," Ella replied.

Dr. King left the room, and Finn took Ella's hand. "How are you doing, sweetheart?"

"I'm okay, but . . ."

"What, love?"

"I've loved being pregnant so much. I know it's a slog for a lot of women and they suffer through it, but it's been the best time of my whole life. I can't even describe how good I've felt, in my body and spirit. The sense of wholeness, oneness—it's inexplicable. Being so close to Betty, it's been better than I ever could have dreamed. I'm a little sad that it's coming to an end. Is that weird?"

He massaged her hand. "I've loved going through every minute of it with you too, so I can only imagine what it's been like for you. But there's not a doubt in my mind that the best is yet to come. We'll finally get to meet our little one; we've dreamed of her for so long."

She smiled and they stared at each other. The moment was broken as Ella started to writhe in pain at another contraction.

"Breathe, baby. Like this," he gently instructed, breathing the way they had been taught in their classes.

When the contraction passed, she fell back onto her pillow. "I'm okay," she said.

Finn kissed her forehead.

Several hours later, Dr. King said, "Four centimeters."

"That's it?" Ella asked, sweating and in pain.

"You're progressing nicely, but like I said, this is going to take time, her being your first baby and all. It will be many hours."

"How do women do this?" Ella groaned.

"We can give you an epidural," Dr. King said. "It will make it easier."

She shook her head. "That's not our plan."

"If you change your mind, let us know. I'll be back to check on you later. You're doing great."

Ella looked at Finn and said, "I've heard so many women say that when they were in labor, they looked at their husbands and thought they'd never want sex again. I never understood."

"Yeah?"

"Well, I do now. The most you can hope for is a blow job from time to time, and even that's getting less likely by the second."

He chuckled. "At least you haven't lost your sense of humor."

"Who says I'm kidding?"

Finn smiled and gently ran a cool compress against her forehead. "You are spectacular, and I love you beyond words."

"I see through your foolish flattery."

He laughed.

Ella's expression turned serious. "Finn, I'm a little worried. This is a lot harder than I thought it would be, and it's taking so long. I'm not even halfway there! I know we have a natural birth plan, but what if I can't do it?"

"Then you'll get the epidural. Plans change. We'll do this any way you want. However you're most comfortable."

"That's not what I want. Please, you have to help . . ." She trailed off, leaned forward, and screamed softly as another contraction came.

When it passed, Finn said, "Do you want me to sit behind you and rub your back? We haven't tried that yet."

She nodded.

He sat behind her, his legs wrapped around her, and massaged her back, whispering sweet affirmations in her ear.

"That feels good," she said.

He kissed the back of her head. "You can do this. I'm here. We're together."

"SEVEN CENTIMETERS? THAT'S ALL? How can that be? It's been eons since I was at four!" Ella howled, flailing back on her pillow and writhing in pain in the sheets drenched with her sweat.

"I know it's hard," Dr. King said, "but you're getting there. Keep it up with the breathing exercises. I'll be back to check on you."

As soon as she left the room, Ella exploded into tears. "I can't do it. I can't do it," she cried.

"Shh . . ." Finn whispered, caressing her forehead. "You are so strong. What you're doing to bring our baby into the world is incredible. I'm in awe. I wish I could take the pain away."

"If I don't make it, promise me you'll make sure Betty is okay," she cried.

"Baby, you're going to get through this. This pain is only temporary."

She shook her head, tears falling uncontrollably from her eyes. "Women die in childbirth all the time. I'm afraid that's what's happening here. That's what it feels like. This doesn't feel right. I'll never even get to meet her," she sobbed, dissolving into hysterics.

"Sweetheart . . ."

"Oh, God!" she screamed, leaning forward as another contraction came.

"Breathe, baby. Breathe," Finn encouraged.

Ella continued wailing until the contraction ended. She looked up at Finn, her face a red, blotchy mess. "Please, you have to listen to me. You have to listen to me."

"I'm listening, sweetheart."

"If there's a choice to be made, save Betty."

"Ella . . ."

"Promise me, Finn. Promise me right now."

"Okay, baby. I promise."

"And if I'm not here to raise her, make sure she knows how much I loved her," she sputtered in between her sobs. "Find out who she is. Let her be her own person. Celebrate her for who she is. Help her to discover her passions and follow them fearlessly, whatever they are. Be patient and kind, even when it's hard. Don't ever break her spirit. Enjoy all the precious moments," she choked out, her tears gushing like a waterfall. "Blue eye shadow. No one ever looks good in blue eyeshadow, but if she paints it all over her eyelids and squeezes herself into spandex, tell her she looks pretty." A smile flickered across his face and he almost laughed, but she continued, "Teach her to have an open heart, to love with everything she has. And you have to love whoever she loves. Make sure she knows that love is all that matters. Promise me, Finn."

"I promise you, baby. I promise," he said, leaning down and kissing her sweaty forehead. "But in my heart, I know you'll be here to teach her all that yourself. Just breathe."

ELLA HAD BEEN PUSHING FOR OVER an hour, beads of sweat dripping from her brow as she gripped Finn's hand.

"Ella, bear down and push. I know you're exhausted, but you're in the home stretch. I need you to push. She's almost here," Dr. King said.

"I can't do it. I can't do it. I have nothing left," Ella muttered. She looked into Finn's eyes, but she was barely able to focus. "I'm sorry. I can't."

"Yes, you can. You can do this. Betty is almost here," he assured her. "Push, Ella. Push."

She pushed as hard as she could.

"I see her head," Dr. King said. "Push, Ella. One more big push."

Ella bore down with all her might, and through an earth-shattering scream, she pushed.

Suddenly, she felt a wave of relief. "Congratulations," Dr. King said just as the room filled with the sound of a newborn's cry. "She's a healthy baby girl."

"Oh my God. She's so tiny, so beautiful," Finn said, choking back tears.

"Here, Dad, you can cut the cord," Dr. King said.

The nurse helped him cut the cord, and then she put the baby on Ella's chest. "Oh, you sweet girl," Ella said, hot tears streaming down her face. She looked at Finn. "You were right. The best was yet to come. She's perfect."

"She sure is," he agreed, rubbing Ella's hair. Washed in a look of love, tears cascaded silently down Finn's face.

"She's so fair. Look, she has your lips," Ella observed.

"And big, beautiful eyes like you."

"But they're blue like yours."

He kissed Ella's forehead, looked deeply into her eyes, and said, "This is the most beautiful sight I've ever seen, the two of you together. Thank you for bringing her into the world. You are spectacular, and I love you with all my heart."

Ella sniffled, looked down at their little bundle, and said, "We love you so much. Welcome to the world, Betty Sinclair Forrester."

CHAPTER 14

Finn peeked into the bathroom. "Hey, girls."

"Daddy!" Betty exclaimed, jumping up and down, her blonde curls bouncing.

"Hey, you," he said, picking her up. "You're getting so big. Are you sure you're only two?" Betty giggled and he asked, "Is it bath time, sweet girl?"

"Daddy, you give me my bath and read my stories."

"Sure," he said, setting her down.

Ella turned the tub off, tested the water one last time, and rose.

"Hi, baby," Finn said, giving her a kiss. "How was your day?"

"It was great. We did a big finger-painting project. Betty really takes after you—planning things out, taking her time, trying to get her art just right. When she's thinking, her eyes get intense like yours too. She's so careful and methodical about selecting each color, and she likes to keep them separate. We may have a budding artist on our hands. Or a mathematician. You'll see her new artwork on the refrigerator."

"I can't wait to see them."

"We had fun, though we made quite a mess."

"Mommy cleaned up," Betty said.

"That's right," Ella replied, pulling off Betty's clothes. "Now it's time to clean you up."

"My turn," Finn insisted. He grazed Ella's arm. "I got this, go relax."

"Joyce roasted a chicken. Meet me at the table when you're done." She bent down and kissed Betty. "Be a good girl for Daddy and have sweet dreams. I'll see you in the morning."

Nearly an hour later, Finn found Ella in the dining room. She began fixing them each a plate of food. "Is she down?"

"Yeah," he replied, dropping a kiss in her hair before taking his seat. "I let her pick three books as always, but then she begged me for one more."

"Finn, if you do that, then . . ."

"I didn't. We just snuggled for a little while. She really loves the touch-and-feel animals book, which is a nice departure from the never-ending princess stories."

"She's so excited for our trip to the zoo tomorrow, and I promised we'd go to the pancake place first. It was funny, though—when I told her we were going to the zoo, she got confused," Ella said. "She thought that meant we were flying to Georgia. I tried to explain that we were just in Georgia for a couple of months while you were making a movie and that there are lots of different zoos in the world, but it went over her head. She had so much fun that day at the Atlanta Zoo."

Finn smiled. "All she wanted was the zebra, and ice cream of course."

"Yeah, I expect we'll be spending most of tomorrow looking at the zebras again. Maybe someday we can take her on a safari in Africa so she can see what they're like out in the wild, where they belong. I want her to know about nature and what the world really looks like."

"Speaking of which, she was telling me about all her body parts again during her bath," Finn said. "Apparently, you taught her a new word. After she found her legs, feet, and toes, she pointed and said, 'gina.' Then she said, 'My gina is mine,' which I guess was her way of saying it's private."

"I think it's important for her to understand her body. Using make-believe words never made sense to me, so I taught her the real word, but she's still learning how to say it, which is kind of cute. I didn't want to tell her not to touch it or shame her for exploring her own body, but I told her it's private and not for other people to touch. It's just hers."

"That's smart. You're such a good mother. Gotta admit, it caught me off guard and I think I stammered a bit. Given the fact that you're the most brilliant and provocative pleasure theorist of our time, I shouldn't have been surprised." She blushed and he continued, "Speaking of which, have you made any progress on your book?"

Ella shook her head. "Barely. Betty takes up most of my time these days. She's at a demanding age. I still manage to attend all of my philosophy club meetings, but I can only find little bits of time to write. Can't remember the last time I could really clear my head and get immersed in it."

"Sweetheart, why don't you use the sitter more?"

"Betty is learning so much every day. Her mind is like a sponge. I'm teaching her how to think, explore, imagine. This is developmental time we can never get back. The book will come."

Finn took her hand, lifted it to his lips, and kissed it. "Like I said, you're such a good mother. If you want more time to write, I can take some of the load off. I don't need to work so much. I'd be happy to be at home with you both."

"It's up to you, but if you're home more, I'd want the three of us to spend that time together," Ella replied. "Like those dreamy months after she was born, when we were all so cozy, just bonding as a little family. We'd go for those long walks, and you would put her in that carrier on your chest, stopping to kiss her head every few minutes. That was the sweetest."

"I wouldn't trade those six months at home for anything. A big part of why I took all that time off was so that you could write, but . . ."

"I was too exhausted. You remember how intense it was. We were up every few hours, and breastfeeding was a full-time job. Besides, I've always believed that the time we spend stewing on things is productive. The book will come. When the time is right, it will come."

"No pressure, but if you want to work more, just say the word and I'll do the stay-at-home-dad thing for as long as you like," Finn said.

"Like I said, I'd love for you to be home more, but I'd want to be with you both every second. There's nothing better. In fact . . ." She trailed off.

"What, baby?"

Ella looked straight into his eyes, took a breath, and said, "I just love our family so much. More than I ever knew was possible."

"Me too. I can't wait to spend tomorrow with my girls."

FINN PAID THE CASHIER AND PICKED up Betty, who was tugging on his jeans. "Did you like those silver dollar pancakes?"

"Yeah. Zoo! Zoo!" she said excitedly.

He smiled and they headed outside. Suddenly, there were two paparazzi snapping photos and screaming, "Finn! Out for a day with your family?"

Finn tried to ignore them, shielding Betty's face as they walked to their car, but the paparazzi persisted, following them and hollering. Betty started crying, leaning her head on his shoulder. "It's okay, sweetheart," he whispered. He strapped her into her car seat, the paparazzi just feet away, still frantically taking photos. He closed the door, turned to them, and said, "What the fuck is wrong with you? That's my kid!" He snapped a photo of their license plate and raced to the driver's side.

Ella was comforting Betty, who was now crying in earnest. She turned to Finn, whose hands were shaking, his face red. "Just drive," she told him.

"It's okay," Ella said softly, handing Betty her favorite stuffed horse. "Everything is okay now. Those people won't bother us again. We're gonna have so much fun today. What animals do you want to see?"

Betty's cries began to slow. She took a few quick breaths and calmed down. "Z . . . z . . . zebra."

"Yay!" Ella said. "We'll see the zebra first, then maybe we can see the giraffes and the elephants."

Betty smiled, gripping her stuffed toy.

"What other animals should we see?" Ella asked.

"Zebra."

Ella laughed. "How about the monkeys?"

"Monkeys and zebras," Betty said.

Ella turned to Finn and gently ran her hand down his arm. He looked at her through a glaze of sadness. "It's okay," she whispered.

When they arrived at the zoo, Finn parked the car and immediately realized they had been followed by the paparazzi. Several more were waiting for them. He turned to Ella and quietly said, "Holy shit. They must have called their friends."

"Maybe we should just go home," she said.

"No way. We promised her. We're not letting these assholes ruin our day. They won't be allowed inside. I'll get Betty and we'll hurry in."

"Finn, it could be more traumatic for her if . . ."

"I'll handle it," he insisted.

"Don't engage with them. It will only make it worse."

He nodded, got out of the car, and walked around to get Betty. "Come to Daddy, sweet girl," he said. The paparazzi started aggressively taking photographs, creating a cacophony of clicking. Finn put his hand on her cheek, trying to shield her face, but she exploded into tears. By the time they reached the ticket counter, Betty was having a complete tantrum, crying hysterically, unable to catch her breath, her head shaking. "It's okay, it's okay," Finn soothed, bouncing her up and down, rubbing her head. Her sobs only worsened. "We can get ice cream," he suggested, but she was totally hysterical, screaming and flailing her arms, her face a blotchy mess.

Ella put her hand on his bicep. "Finn, let's take her home. Please, we need to go now."

With a look of rage on his face, he carried Betty back to the car, glaring at the heartless photo hounds. He strapped her into her car seat, and Ella slipped into the back seat beside her. They drove home, Betty sobbing hysterically the whole way. When they got to the house, Finn tried to take Betty out of the car, but she pulled away and screamed, "Mommy! Mommy!"

"It's okay. I've got her," Ella told him.

"Come here, little one," she said, picking Betty up. She completely collapsed on Ella's chest. "It's okay. It's okay. You can let it out. You'll feel better soon," Ella whispered, rubbing Betty's back as her cries slowed.

When they got inside, Ella said, "I'm going to try to put her down for a nap." Finn watched them disappear upstairs, his shoulders slumped, his heart broken.

Half an hour later, Ella wandered into the den with the baby monitor and found Finn lying on the couch, a cigarette in one hand, a framed photo in the other. "How is she?" he asked, stamping out his butt.

"Fine. She's finally sleeping," Ella replied, lying beside him.

"This is my favorite photograph," he said, looking wistfully at the photo of Ella breastfeeding Betty. "I'll never forget that moment. I was right here, you were sitting over there on that rug with Betty in your lap, and we were talking. She got fussy, so you pulled your tank top down on one side and she latched onto you. It was so beautiful, effortless. I just had to capture it. I love how you can only see your spectacular mane of curls that are covering your face, and Betty's eyes looking at the camera, her mouth on you, and the shape of your perfect breast with that sweet little beauty mark above it." He stopped to shake his head. "You just went right on having a conversation with me, but I could hardly hear a word. I was so overcome with love, watching my beautiful family."

"That's so sweet."

He put the frame down and draped his arm over her. "When I look at that photo and compare it in my mind with the times you've been exploited because of me . . ."

"Finn, that's ridiculous."

"Don't you remember the yacht? I couldn't believe the paparazzi got those long-lens photos of you sunbathing topless. They have no shame."

She shrugged. "At the end of the day, I didn't care. I was sunbathing with my husband. Besides, I'm not ashamed of my body."

"You have the most beautiful breasts I've ever seen, but to see you objectified in that way, without your consent," Finn said, shaking his head. "I'm to blame. This is all my fault."

"Finn . . ."

"And that time when Betty was only a few months old and they somehow got photos of us on that park bench when you were breastfeeding. Watching you nurture our child is the most tender thing I've ever seen. To see it exploited . . ."

"That was gross and it upset me too, but again, who really cares? Her face was blurred in the magazines. Sure, there have been a few unpleasant incidents over the years, but that's it. It isn't our daily life."

"Ella, I'm so sorry about today," he said, hanging his head.

"You have nothing to apologize for."

"It's my fault."

"Don't be absurd," Ella replied. "Those paparazzi are scum; today was on them. They should have been arrested. There are laws against tormenting children like that."

"I called my lawyer while you were putting Betty down. The photos will never see the light of day. They'll be hit with a restraining order, probably some hefty fines. But it doesn't matter. It doesn't undo anything or reduce the likelihood of this happening again." He stopped to shake his head. "It's all my fault."

"Finn, that's ridiculous."

"They were harassing us because of me," he said. "Betty knew it. She wouldn't even let me take her out of the car. She only wanted you."

"Sometimes she only wants you. It doesn't mean anything. By the time she wakes up, she'll probably be begging for her daddy again."

"The way she was crying, screaming, her whole body violently shaking—she could hardly catch her breath. I felt her pain, her sense of violation, in the deepest part of my soul. It gutted me."

"Kids her age have tantrums for all kinds of reasons," Ella said. "Don't you remember last month? She had a complete meltdown leaving that birthday party. She was inconsolable."

Finn let out a puff. "You were amazing, like always. The screaming was getting to me, but you never lost your patience. The way you validated how she was feeling, told her it's hard when fun things end and that it's okay to be upset, told her to let it out, all while you cradled her shaking body. God, you're such a good mother."

She smiled. "My point is that kids her age lose it sometimes."

"Maybe, but what happened today was because of me. I brought this shit into her life and yours. She never signed up for it. Your mother was right."

"What are you talking about?"

"The first time I met her, she called me out for how I proposed. Regardless of my intentions, it was a spectacle. I created an insatiable public interest in our private life. This fucking circus." He shook his head. "Even if I hadn't proposed publicly, this kind of thing happens when you're famous. That's on me. Ella, I was irresponsible. When I chose this line of work, I never thought about what fame might mean if I ever had a family, how people would violate our privacy as if we aren't even human, how that would impact my wife, my kids."

"Finn, look at me." He raised his gaze to meet hers. "Today was an aberration. We usually don't have these kinds of problems."

"Watching the people you love the most get hurt because of your choices . . ."

"You can only live your life; you can't control anything else. What happened today wasn't your fault."

"I couldn't protect her."

"That's not true," Ella protested. "You did the best you could under the circumstances. And I have news for you: this won't be the last time you feel that way. No parent can protect their child from everything. Someday it will be a scraped knee, or a bully on the playground, or her first love will break her heart. We'll stand by helplessly, just trying to comfort her until she recovers."

He inhaled deeply. "Maybe, but I can do something about this kind of thing. I've made a decision. I'm quitting acting."

"Finn . . ."

"Hear me out. This has been in the back of my mind since those breastfeeding photos were splashed across the covers of those rags. I've been acting professionally since I was a teenager, and I've had more success than I ever imagined. It's been a great run. I'll quit, we'll leave LA, and we'll slip under the radar. Some celebrities move to places like Montana. I've heard it's beautiful up there. We could do that."

"Oh, Finn," she said, running her thumb against his temple. "Being an artist isn't something you can just stop. You can't disavow who you are. You're an actor, a deeply talented and gifted one at that. Most importantly, you love your work. You can't give up such a big part of who you are for—"

"Yes, I can. For you, for Betty. To give her a shot at a normal life. I love you both more than anything. I'll do whatever it takes. Family first. Today was unbearable. I never want to see her that way again."

Ella planted a delicate kiss on his lips. "You're understandably upset over what happened. It's still so fresh and raw. Trust me, Betty will be fine. The best thing you can do for her is to continue to be a role model. Let her see you living your best life, doing what you love with everything you have, and loving her with all your heart. Let love be your guide, not fear." She gave him another gentle kiss. "We made a pact. I won't allow you to lose yourself. I love you too much." He smiled and ran his finger along her hairline. She continued, "Besides, what *is* a normal life, anyway? Let's give her an extraordinary life."

"I love you so much," he said, pressing his mouth to hers.

"I love you too, more than I can say. Finn, you're a magnificent father. Our babies are so lucky to have you."

He furrowed his brow. "Babies?"

She smiled as tears welled in her eyes. "I found out yesterday. I was going to tell you at the zoo. I had this vision of sharing the news while we were getting ice cream. We're having another baby. I'm pregnant."

"Oh, sweetheart," Finn said, his eyes flooding. He kissed her softly and rested his forehead against hers. "I'm so happy, I don't even have the words."

"It must have happened when we started trying in Georgia. We got lucky and conceived quickly again."

"Like I've said for years, we were made to make babies together," he said.

She pulled back and looked deeply into his eyes. "There's no one else in the world I'd want to do this with. You're the most incredible man and the best father our children could ever have. Please be you, full fucking throttle."

He laughed and kissed the tip of her nose. "Let's just lie here like this, holding each other, feeling every bit of this moment."

CHAPTER 15

"**S**ocrates basically argued that love was bullshit. He was fancier about it, so I'm paraphrasing," Marni said as the others laughed. "But I'm serious. He philosophized that we only want what we can't have, and thus it's always fleeting, never deep. I know this puts me in the minority in our romance-obsessed culture, but I think he was on to something."

"Of course you do," Ella replied with a giggle.

Marni shrugged and helped herself to another stuffed grape leaf off the Greek meze platter Ella had prepared for their meeting. "These are delicious. The hummus too. I so love it when you host our club. I'm the worst."

"Nonsense. Who doesn't enjoy stale crackers and tap water? And so clever to use toilet paper in lieu of napkins," Ella joked.

Jade laughed, covering her mouth.

Dante looked at Marni. "When you're done gorging yourself, try to remember that we're supposed to be inspiring Ella for her book project. Your gloom and doom is more likely to put her off the whole thing."

"First of all, you went to town on that olive tapenade," Marni rebuffed, giving him the side-eye. "Second, what can I say? I'm a realist. Besides, take a look around. We're basically having this discussion in Prince Charming's castle, and Ella's growing another one of his love children as we speak. I don't think she's falling off the romantic love bandwagon anytime soon."

Ella smiled and touched her belly. "Fear not, I am resistant to the pessimism. These days, I feel especially hopeful."

"That may be the pregnancy hormones talking," Marni quipped.

Ella smirked.

"I'm a terrible friend, I admit it. Seriously, how have you been feeling?" Marni asked.

"Never better. I can feel our little one fluttering around. I've hardly had the time to write a thing because I want to give Betty as much attention as possible before she has to share me, but I do feel inspired. It's strange because I used to think of love as something we want for ourselves, but now . . ."

Marni raised her eyebrows.

"I'm not sure. All I do know is that I feel consumed by love, and it's all directed at my family. Being with them, nurturing them, experiencing life with them." Ella crinkled her nose and shook her head. "It's the way I feel most alive."

"Sounds like you're an Aristotle girl. He believed that love requires us to focus on what is best for the other, not ourselves. There's nobility in that, beauty," Dante said.

"But to do that, he believed we must first love ourselves so that we can best love others," Jade added.

"Ah, finally something I can get behind," Marni said. She turned to Ella and asked, "What do you think?"

"Wouldn't that create a dialectical? If we focus on what's best for those we love, then they would simultaneously be focusing on what's best for us. It's reciprocal," Ella said.

"When you cut through it all, the question becomes: Is love about focusing on what's best for others, or should self-love come before all else?" Marni said.

"Maybe that's not really the question." Ella leaned back on the sofa. "Perhaps it's more complicated. I think the question is: When it comes to love, is it even a question of self and other, or something else entirely?"

 CHAPTER 16

"Ella, where are you?" Finn called as he came through the door one afternoon.

"Up here," she replied.

Finn bounded up the stairs and found her in their bedroom closet. "Hi, sweetheart," he said.

"Hey, you," she said, smiling brightly.

"What are you doing?"

"Organizing the closet. Now that I'm well into my third trimester," she replied, patting her growing belly, "it's time to give up the ghost and put the crop tops in the back. The maternity dresses and jumpers belong up front."

He smiled faintly. "Where's Betty?"

"At a playdate. The sitter should be bringing her home in about an hour. I'm a bit surprised to see you; you're back from the meeting with your agent kind of early."

He took a deep breath and said, "I need to talk to you, sweetheart."

"What's wrong?" she asked, her expression turning serious.

"Come here, love," he said, taking her hand and leading her to the love seat.

"Finn, you're scaring me. What's wrong?"

"Nothing, baby," he said, stroking her cheek. "Two days ago, a man claiming to be your father contacted my agent in an attempt to get in touch with you." Her eyes went wide as he continued, "I didn't want to say anything until we had confirmed whether it was really him. His story checks out. He's your father."

"Oh my God," she mumbled. Her eyes fell to her lap and she sat perfectly still, processing what she'd heard. After a long moment passed, she looked into Finn's eyes and asked, "Do you know what he wants?"

"Only that he wants to see you. He claims he's been trying to get in touch with you for over a year. His messages probably got mixed up with my fan mail."

"Do you have a way to contact him?"

Finn reluctantly pulled a piece of paper out of his pocket and handed it to her. "That's his cell phone number. Ella, are you actually thinking about reaching out?"

"I . . . I . . ." He cupped her cheek and she said, "I'm in shock. But . . ."

"What, love?"

"He's my father. If he wants to see me . . ."

"Sweetheart, he abandoned you. Why would you give him the time of day?"

"I don't know the whole story, only what my mother has told me. Maybe there's another side to it."

"As a father, I can't see how. There's no circumstance under which I wouldn't be in my child's life. It's incomprehensible. Inexcusable."

"For all we know, my mother pushed him away," Ella said. "We always moved around a lot, so maybe he didn't even know where to find me when I was growing up."

"Then why hasn't he gotten in touch with you in all the years since?"

"Maybe he tried to. My mother could have prevented him, or . . ."

"Ella," he whispered.

"What? Why won't you give him the benefit of the doubt?" She paused as her eyes welled up. "You don't know what it's like. You have two wonderful parents who have always been there for you," she said as she began to cry. "Our children have that too. Why won't you give me a chance to have even a little bit of that?"

"Baby, I told you about this as soon as we confirmed it's him. I'm not preventing anything, but . . ."

"It's like you're poisoning it from the start, like you can't see how this could be a good thing. A gift. For me, for our kids."

"Honestly, I'm surprised," Finn said. "This isn't the reaction I expected. I didn't think you'd want anything to do with him. You've never been . . ."

"What? A pushover?"

"No, baby. You're just so shrewd and discerning. You expect a lot from people, and rightfully so. Trust has always been hard-earned for you. Hell, you didn't even trust me in the beginning."

"Maybe I'm different now. Being with you, our kids," she said, holding her belly. "I don't know how to just clamp off my feelings anymore. They leak. When you open your heart, it's not so easy to close it again, and I'm not sure I'd want to."

He looked at her lovingly and caressed her cheek. "Sweetheart, it's just . . ."

"What?" she asked.

"Of all the ways he could have gotten in touch with you, he did it through my agent."

"So?"

"Doesn't that strike you as suspicious?"

"Maybe it's the only way he could find me."

"Baby, he could have reached out to your mother or your publisher," Finn said. "The fact that he went through my agent makes me question his motives. He didn't get in touch with you for decades, but now, when he obviously knows we're married . . ."

"You think this is because you're famous?"

"I've been through this kind of thing before. Fame and money are very seductive to a lot of people. Celebrity can lure all types to come crawling out of the woodwork. I would feel terrible if that's what's happening here."

"We don't know that it is. Besides, the whole world has known about our relationship for years. If fame were the lure, don't you think he would have tried to contact me after our engagement or our wedding?" Ella said. "Both were splashed across newspapers and magazines around the world. We were kind of hard to avoid for a while there."

"There could be a reason why he waited until now, something he wants. Who knows? The whole thing makes me uneasy."

"Finn, he's my father. If there's any chance that he sincerely wants me in his life . . ."

"Ella . . ."

"Please just leave me alone," she said, rising.

"Sweetheart," he said, taking her hand.

She let go. "Please. I need some time by myself."

Finn stood up and gave her a peck. "I'm sorry if I said something wrong. I'm only trying to look out for you. I love you."

"I know."

AFTER HE LEFT THE ROOM, ELLA wandered over to her keepsake chest. She opened it and retrieved the teddy bear her father had given her the last time she saw him. She crawled into bed, holding the ragged toy close to her body and trying to breathe.

An hour later, there was a tap on the door. Ella turned to look as Finn walked in with Betty in his arms. "Someone came home and wanted to see you," he said.

"Mommy!" Betty exclaimed.

"Come here, sweet girl," she said.

"Let's have a family snuggle," Finn suggested, climbing into bed and putting Betty between them.

"Did you have fun?" Ella asked.

Betty nodded enthusiastically. "We made rainbow cookies and played dress-up. I was a princess. My dress was blue."

"That sounds like fun," Ella said.

"Ooh, teddy bear," Betty said, grabbing the plush toy. "Mine."

"Sweetheart, that's special to your mommy," Finn explained. "Let's give it back to her, and after we snuggle, we can get a teddy bear from your room. Okay?"

"Okay," Betty agreed with a little pout, releasing the toy.

Ella looked at Finn and mouthed, "Thank you."

"ARE YOU SURE YOU DON'T WANT ME to go with you?" Finn asked.

"I'm sure," Ella replied, slinging her handbag on her shoulder.

"If it's because of how I reacted yesterday, then . . ."

"It's not."

"I'm worried about you," Finn said.

"I can take care of myself."

He took her hand, caressing her skin. "Baby, you haven't seen your father in over thirty years. That would be a lot for anyone, no matter the circumstances. It has the potential to be . . ." He trailed off, as if the words alluded him.

"What?" she asked.

"Emotional. Stressful." He shook his head. "I don't know what, and you don't either. How could you?"

"Finn, he's my father and he wants to reconnect, maybe get to know me. Besides, it's just lunch at a diner. I'll be fine. Please stop poisoning it."

"That's not what I'm trying to do. I'm just concerned. I'm afraid he's going to hurt you, disappoint you. Every part of me is screaming to protect you. Ella, you're pregnant. I'm worried that if it's upsetting—"

"Finn, please. The baby and I will be fine," Ella insisted. "You're only acting this way because you've already made up your mind that he's a dirtbag who doesn't really care about me, that he's only using me. I'm choosing to be hopeful, choosing to have an open heart. I have to go or I'll be late."

He put his hand on her cheek and gave her a gentle kiss. "I'll be here for anything you need. From the bottom of my heart, I hope it goes the way you want it to. You deserve only good things, Ella. I love you."

ELLA WALKED THROUGH THE RESTAURANT door, the chime ringing in her ears as her pulse quickened. She immediately spotted her father sitting in a booth by the window, nervously running his hand through his dyed brown hair. Her heart continued to race as she approached, and he rose to greet her.

"Hi. Wow," he said, doing a double take. "You look so much like your mother in person, even more than in photos."

"Hi," she said. "I'm not sure what to do, or even what to call you."

He put one hand on her shoulder and gave her an awkward peck on the cheek. They sat down opposite each other. "Call me Bruce," he said.

A waitress came over and asked, "Can I get you something to drink, honey?"

"An orange juice, please," Ella replied.

"Coffee for me, black," Bruce added. He turned to Ella and said, "It's hard to know where to begin."

"Why did you leave?" He looked at her blankly, as if totally unprepared for the question. "I'm sorry," she said. "I didn't mean to blurt that out, but . . ."

"Carmen and I . . ."

"My mother."

"Yes. Your mother and I ended our relationship. She's a very seductive woman. I didn't know what hit me when we met. The affair came out of left field. It was a fiery relationship from the start. Lust. Passion. Eventually, that faded. Plus . . ." He got quiet as the waitress delivered their drinks.

"Are you two ready to order?" the waitress asked.

"We need some time, please," Ella replied. She looked at Bruce. "You were saying."

"The relationship just naturally fizzled with Carmen, your mother. Plus, I was married. I needed to try to make it work with my wife."

"But why did you leave *me*?" she asked.

He squirmed a bit before saying, "You had your mother. My wife and kids needed me."

Her eyes fell to her lap and she leaned back in her seat, away from him. "I was your kid too," she mumbled.

"Yes, but you know what I mean. I had never lived with you. You didn't depend on me, like my family did."

Ella took a sip of her juice to buy a moment to gather her thoughts. "How many kids do you have?"

"Two. My daughter is five years older than you, and my son is—well, he's just about your age."

"So, you were . . ."

"Sleeping with my wife when I was seeing your mother. It was complicated. We're all grown-ups. I'm sure you can understand."

She shook her head as if trying to make sense of what she was hearing. "You said you have two kids. I guess that's how you think about it, but you have three. You have me too."

"Yes, of course. But you know what I mean. Two kids I raised."

"Do they know about me? Do they know they have a half sister?"

Bruce sighed. "My wife never found out about the affair with your mother, so . . ."

"I see," she said.

"Would you like to see pictures of them?" he asked. Ella nodded, and he scrolled through his cell phone before handing it to her. "That's my daughter with her husband and their two kids. The next one is my son. Still a bachelor."

She slid the phone back to him. "So, you have grandkids."

"Yes, lights of my life."

Ella's eyes began to well up, but she used all her might to hold it in.

Bruce reached his hand across the table and put it over hers. She flinched a little but didn't pull away. "Look, Ella, I know I wasn't there for you when you were growing up. I'm sorry you didn't have a proper father figure and for the pain that must have caused. I'd like to be in your life now. I was hoping we could get to know each other, maybe become friends, if you're willing to give me a chance. I could even try to be a father to you if that's something you'd like." She took a breath. "How far along are you?" he asked.

"About thirty weeks," she replied, rubbing her belly. "We're having a girl. Her name is Georgia. She was conceived when my husband was working outside of Atlanta, so when we found out I was pregnant, we started calling the baby our little Georgia peach. When we learned she's a girl, the name Georgia was the natural choice. Our daughter Betty is two and three-quarters. She's very specific about her age. She's excited to be a big sister."

"That's a great age. My oldest couldn't wait for her little brother, but then she got jealous once he came." Ella smiled half-heartedly. "Do you have a picture of Betty?" he asked.

"Sure," she replied, reaching for her cell phone. She opened an album of family photos, and he zipped through them.

"She's beautiful. She has curls just like you and your mother, but so blonde," he said. "Tell me about her."

"She's a lot like her father. She's a romantic, obsessed with fairy tales and make believe, and she loves art. They're both very thoughtful about things too, whereas I'm more spontaneous. It's funny because I was in labor with her forever. Now that I know her, I'm convinced she was just taking her time. I can already tell that Georgia has a different personality. Sometimes when I get the hiccups, she gets them too, totally out of sync with mine. Something tells me she's got a good sense of humor. I'm wondering whether she'll be more like me," she said, touching her belly. "But if they both take after their father, I won't complain."

"He's a terrific actor. I've seen many of his films."

"He loves performing, storytelling."

"I'd love to meet him sometime. Actually, I have a business venture he might be interested in. I'm investing in a chain of modern karaoke bars throughout Asia. We've been looking for another investor, and a spokesperson."

Ella's heart sank. She couldn't move and could hardly breathe.

The waitress returned and asked, "Are you two ready to order?"

"My daughter first. Ella, what are you having?" Bruce said.

FINN AND BETTY WERE SITTING ON THE floor playing when Ella walked through the front door. "Mommy's home!" Betty said.

Finn looked up and saw the anguish in Ella's eyes. She looked at them both and then quickly scurried upstairs without a word.

A few minutes later, after setting Betty up to watch a cartoon, Finn went upstairs, letting himself into their bedroom. Ella was lying in bed, crying softly. He crawled behind her and draped his arm over her. "I'm here, baby," he whispered, kissing the back of her head.

"You were right," she whimpered.

"I'm so sorry, sweetheart. I'm so sorry."

"He doesn't care about me at all," she sputtered in between her cries. "He hasn't thought about me in all these years, probably not even once. He was only interested in getting to you, to use your celebrity for some stupid business venture."

Finn inhaled deeply. "I'm so sorry."

Ella sniffled and said, "It was so humiliating. Worst of all, I just sat there like a fool. I didn't want him to see how hurt I was. And I was too embarrassed to come home and face you."

"Oh, baby. You have nothing to be embarrassed about. I'm so sorry I made you feel that way. Please, let me see your face." She turned toward him, and he used his thumbs to gently wipe away the wetness under her eyes. "Ella, I was wrong. What you did today was incredibly courageous. I'm in awe of you. There's nothing to regret now because you were brave enough to lead with an open heart. I hope our girls are just like you."

"Wow, you really are a good actor."

"Oh, sweetheart," he said, cradling her in his embrace.

CHAPTER 17

Ella was lying on the couch in her office, staring at the ceiling, when there was a knock on the door.

"Come in," she said despondently.

"Hey, hey, hey!" Marni said, sauntering in with a brown paper bag in hand.

"Hey. I'm surprised to see you," Ella said, sitting up.

"Finn let me in. He and Betty are watching some fairy-tale movie. It looked brutal. The best part is that she's dressed up in a princess costume, complete with wand, and your husband is wearing a tiara that looks like it was made out of aluminum foil. Poor bastard."

Ella smiled half-heartedly. "What are you doing here?"

"Well, you've skipped philosophy club for the last three weeks, so I figured I'd come over and we'd have a private meeting. I brought snacks," Marni explained, placing a bottle of wine, water, a baguette, cheese, and salami on the tea table. "Here, I even brought paper plates and cups," she said, removing them from the bag. "Impressed?"

"Very," Ella replied. "You know I'm pregnant, right? I can't drink."

"The wine is for me."

"It's not even noon."

"It's rosé," Marni said with a shrug. "So, how are you feeling?" she asked, preparing them each a plate of food.

"Fine. Georgia kicks a lot," Ella said, touching her tummy.

"How's the book coming? Have you been writing?"

"Marni, what are you really doing here?"

Marni sighed. "Finn called me, asked me to pop by."

"Why would he do that?"

"Because he's worried about you, dummy. He said you've been really depressed for the last few weeks since you saw your deadbeat dad."

"It was not his place to call you."

"Babe, the guy loves you. Like gaga, over-the-moon kind of love, and you know me—I'm not even a believer in that horseshit." Ella smiled faintly and Marni continued, "He said you seem sad all the time. You don't laugh. You're not working. You take care of Betty, but . . ."

"What?" she asked defensively.

"Just that you don't seem joyful, even with her. It's so unlike you, Ella."

"I'm doing my best. Being criticized doesn't help."

"No one is criticizing you in the least. He only wants you to be happy."

"No one's happy all the time."

"You're telling me!" Marni said. "Well, maybe those real housewife zombie plastic things."

Ella smiled.

"Ah, a real smile. We're making progress!" Marni said.

Ella looked down. She took a moment and said, "I feel so lost."

"Talk to me."

"Five years ago, if my father had called, I would have told him to fuck off without a moment's hesitation. There's no way I would have given him the time of day. But now, I don't know, it was like my mind was instantly made up to give him a chance. Finn knew the score. He tried to warn me, but it just hurt my feelings."

"Who are you upset with, your father or Finn?"

"Neither. It's not about them. It's about me. Marni, I have no clue who I am anymore. Who is this stupid girl that gets a call from her deadbeat dad and goes running off, hoping for some kind of made-for-television movie reunion? As if he'd been writing me letters my whole life and I'd just never gotten them."

"Someone kind and generous, that's who," Marni replied. "Just because you're way too good for that son of a bitch doesn't mean you aren't exactly who you're supposed to be."

Ella sat quietly for a moment. "Do you remember when I first moved to LA and you told me not to let love change me?"

Marni nodded.

"It has. Since I met Finn and we decided to build a life together and have a family," she said, placing her hand on her belly, "I'm different."

"Ella, when I said that thing about changing, I only meant not to lose yourself. I didn't mean don't change at all. Fuck, everyone changes. As for romantic love and all that hooey, as far as I can see, Finn has made you *more* of who you are, not less. These past few years, you've been happier, more grounded, and freer than you ever were before. That's because of Finn and these rug rats you're popping out."

Ella smiled. "I love them so much. I do. It's just . . ."

"Tell me."

Ella took a breath. "When we love so deeply, it's like it changes our DNA or something. We start to see everyone differently. We move through the world differently." She stopped to shake her head. "It's hard to explain. I don't want to be someone who takes that call from her deadbeat dad, but at the same time, I don't know how not to be her. Not anymore."

"You know, this is the philosopher in you," Marni said. "Some of us have a shitty experience and we stick our head in a tub of ice cream and call it a day. But you've always asked the big questions, of both the world and of yourself. Maybe instead of moping and wallowing, you can use this as fuel. Hell, you're writing a treatise about love. That's some complex shit. Take a deep dive on paper. See where it takes you."

"I haven't written a word in weeks. Honestly, I'm not even sure if I'm going to finish the book at all. Writing about love doesn't seem like such a good idea anymore. I can't even bring myself to open my laptop."

"Give it time. The pieces of the book you've written so far are amazing. Best work of your career. Take a break if you need to, but don't abandon it."

Ella shrugged. "The book is supposed to be about what happens when we love. I was trying to figure out where we end and where the other person begins. When Finn and I first fell in love, I couldn't bring myself to take the leap. I was terrified about what might happen to me if I allowed myself to truly love him, so I pushed him away. When we got back together, I let go of that fear and opened my whole heart. It's like I stopped worrying about my borders and leaned into the closeness. Finn did too." She paused and then added, "We had a little scare when I was pregnant with Betty. You should have seen him, the fear in his eyes, his attachment to us both. He said my pregnancy fundamentally changed something inside of him. Marni, that's what love does. It changes us at an almost cellular level, and now . . ." She took a breath and said, "Now I don't know where my borders are."

"Ella, if you don't know who you are, if you feel lost, turn to the thing that has always been inside of you. You're a philosopher who is chasing the big questions. Go there. That's how you'll find yourself again."

"Thanks. Maybe. We'll see."

"Okay, I'll leave it alone for the time being," Marni said. "Come on, let's stuff ourselves silly on bread and cheese. You've got that basketball of a stomach right now to cover a multitude of sins. Let's put it to good use."

CHAPTER 18

"Finn, wake up," Ella said, shaking him.

"What is it?" he asked groggily.

"My water broke."

"What?" he asked, leaping up. "You're not due for three more weeks."

"Tell that to the baby. She's tired of waiting."

"Oh my God," Finn said, noticing the wet sheets. He started spinning around in circles, unable to decide what to do first. "Wait right there, sweetheart. I'll throw some clothes on, and then I'll help you get dressed. What time is it?" he asked, turning to the clock without waiting for an answer. "Just after five. I'll need to call the sitter, or Jason, or someone to watch Betty until my parents can get here. And Dr. King, we'll call her when we're on our way. Don't worry, baby, everything is okay."

Ella giggled. "You might want to tell yourself that. Relax, my love. Our little one is coming."

He took a breath, kissed her forehead, and said, "You caught me off guard, but I've got this."

"It seems Georgia may take after me. Clearly, she's spontaneous, and I get the feeling she's having a good laugh at throwing her daddy into a frenzy."

"ELLA, THE BABY IS CROWNING; there's no time to get you to labor and delivery. She's coming now," Dr. King said, peering up from between Ella's legs.

"But we just got here. I don't . . ."

"Your child is ready. Push, Ella, push!"

Finn and Ella exchanged a shocked look. He took her hand, and she bore down and pushed.

"One more big push," Dr. King said.

Ella pushed with all her might, letting out a primal shriek.

"Your daughter is here," Dr. King announced, holding the newborn.

"How is she?" Finn asked. At that moment, the baby let out her first cry.

"She's perfect. Here, you can cut the cord, Dad."

"I love you so much, sweet little girl," Finn whispered as he cut the cord.

The doctor placed the baby in her mother's arms.

"My God, she's so beautiful," Finn said. "She looks just like you. The spitting image."

Ella burst into tears, unable to formulate words.

Finn leaned down and planted a tiny kiss on the tip of her nose. "Thank you, sweetheart. Thank you for bringing this angel into the world."

Ella's tears kept falling as she looked down at their newest little love.

"Are you okay, baby?" Finn asked.

She smiled and said, "I had forgotten what it feels like to be this happy."

A FEW DAYS LATER, ELLA WAS NURSING Georgia in her bed at home, with Betty and Finn beside her. Betty gently patted Georgia's head.

"That's a good girl," Ella said.

"I'm the big sister," Betty declared.

"That's right," Finn said. "See how Mommy feeds her? She did the same thing for you."

"Did you feed me too?" she asked, looking up at her father.

"This is something that a mommy does for her baby. When you were old enough for a bottle and big-girl food, I fed you."

"She's real hungry, my sister," Betty observed, intrigued by the process.

Ella smiled and held the newborn to her chest. She patted her back until Georgia let out a little burp.

Betty giggled. "'Scuse you!"

Ella cradled the baby in her arms. Betty watched and said, "Look, she smiled! My baby sister smiled."

Finn rubbed her back. "She's a little too young to smile. It does look like that, but she probably just had a little gas."

"Look. Look," Betty insisted. "She smiled again."

"You know what, I think Betty's right. I think our Georgia peach is already smiling at us," Ella said. As she looked down at the funny faces Georgia was making, she began to laugh. Her laughter got louder, and soon she was completely overtaken by the giggles.

"Silly Mommy," Betty said.

Ella finally caught her breath and said, "I guess sometimes I'm silly." She gazed over at Finn and asked, "Would you mind watching them?"

"Of course not," he replied as she passed the baby.

Ella kissed Betty's forehead and said, "Please be Daddy's helper." She slipped out of bed and put her robe on.

"What are you doing?" Finn asked.

"Going to my office to write."

"That's great! You haven't worked in months," he replied.

"Suddenly, I feel inspired," Ella said. "Come get me if she gets fussy."

"Come here and give me a kiss first," he said. She walked over and gave him a smooch. "We'll be fine. Take all the time you want. Do your thing."

Ella smiled and headed to her office. Walking into the magnificent room, she stopped to take it all in and see it anew: the sparkling Eiffel Tower, the old map of Sweden, the books, the photos, the globe they had examined each time Finn booked a job on location. She crossed the room to her laptop, turned it on, and took a slow, deep, deliberate breath. She began skimming the notes she had been compiling for years, then opened a blank document and typed a single word: *love.*

CHAPTER 19

Standing in front of the open patio doors in her office, Ella was thinking about how quickly the last year had flown by: Georgia, the comedian of the household, was running around at full toddler speed. Betty, now four, was coming more into her own each day. While she still had a ways to go, her book had finally taken shape and was more than halfway done. Suddenly, a knock on her office door jarred her back into the present. "Come in."

"I hope I'm not disturbing you," Joyce said as she stepped into the room.

"Not in the slightest. I love how the air changes at the start of autumn. I was just soaking it up. Are the girls back from their playdate at the orchard?"

"No, but I expect the sitter will bring them back any time now. If they come home with bags of apples, what would you like to do with them?"

"Oh, I was thinking I'd teach them how to make applesauce, and maybe a pie or muffins, depending on how many apples they have."

"Let me know if I can help. I just came to drop this off," Joyce said, handing her a piece of mail.

"Thank you," Ella replied. Joyce closed the door behind her as she left, and Ella looked down at the return address. She inhaled deeply, then tore open the envelope, removed the letter, and quietly read it aloud.

"Dear Ms. Sinclair, Congratulations! The University of Cambridge is pleased to inform you that you have been chosen as our Spring Philosophy Fellow . . ." Her eyes instantly welled up. She took a breath, gazed around her beautiful office, a big room designed to inspire big ideas, looked back down at the letter she clutched in her hand, and stood perfectly still, savoring the moment.

The quiet was broken with another knock on the door. Joyce peeked her head in. "Sorry to disturb you again. The sitter just pulled up with the girls."

Ella blinked away her tears of joy and slipped the letter into her pocket. "On my way."

A few hours later, Ella and the girls were in the backyard playing ring-around-the-rosy. They all tumbled to the ground just as Finn approached the joyful scene.

"Well, this is a cheery sight. How are my girls?" he asked.

Betty jumped up and ran over to him, tugging his hand to come join the fun. Georgia stood up and started shaking with excitement from her head to her toes. "Dada! Dada!" she screeched, her little toddler body unable to contain her unabashed joy.

"Hello, little peach," he said, scooping her up, tickling her belly, and kissing the top of her head. He carefully set her down and gave Ella a delicate kiss. "Hi, love. How was your day?"

"It was great. The girls had a blast at the orchard. You should probably start calling Georgia your little ham instead of your little peach. I heard she was a riot at the playdate, trying to make everyone laugh, as usual. I also heard Betty was an angel, helping all the little ones. We made all kinds of treats with the apples they brought back. Oh, and I have something to tell—"

"Dada! Dada!" Georgia said, pulling on his pants, then tugging at his hand.

"I think she wants you to take a spin with us," Ella said with a wink.

They all held hands and sang "Ring Around the Rosy," toppling to the ground in laughter. The girls crawled on top of Finn, Georgia giggling hysterically and Betty blabbering a mile a minute about their apple-picking excursion. "We made a pie too. Mommy said we can have it with ice cream for dessert," Betty said.

"Speaking of ice cream, I have some pretty big news," Finn announced. He looked at Ella lying in the grass beside them and asked, "How would you feel about spending a couple of months in Italy?"

She raised her eyebrows.

Georgia squealed.

Finn laughed, picked up Georgia, and held her up in the air above his body. "We might just be going to Italy to have gelato."

"'Lato!" Georgia repeated.

"What's that, Daddy?" Betty asked.

"It's the best ice cream in the world. I like chocolate, and your mommy likes mint chocolate chip," he said, glancing over at Ella. "What flavors do you think you'll try?"

"Strawberry and vanilla," Betty said thoughtfully.

"So, what's this all about?" Ella asked.

"I was offered the lead in a film with a director I've been itching to work with. It's shooting in Rome in March and April. How fantastic is that?" Ella smiled faintly and he continued, "With Betty starting school next September, this is the last time we can take advantage of a location shoot outside of summers. What do you think?"

Ella looked at him holding their girls, both bursting with joy, so much love and affection between them all. Suddenly, she saw flashes of their life, like a film reeling through her mind: the soul-shattering hurt on his face when she ended their relationship, the hope in his eyes when he proposed, the curve of his lips when he read a script in bed, the first sonogram image of Betty, the resolve in his eyes when he contemplated quitting acting, Betty sound asleep on his chest, Georgia safe in his arms. Ella swore she could still feel his breath on her cheek the first time they danced, his fingers woven into her hair after they made love, the warmth of his arm around her pregnant belly when she lay in bed crying, his kiss on the back of her head. As the feelings took hold, it was as if there was a soundtrack to the film in her mind. She could hear the sound of their cries when Betty was born, and Georgia's insatiable laughter.

As the vision faded, Finn touched her hand. "Ella? You look like you're a million miles away. What do you say to Italy, baby?"

She swallowed the lump in her throat and softly said, "It sounds great."

A FEW DAYS LATER, FINN WAS GETTING a glass of water when Marni walked into the kitchen.

"Hey," he said. She glanced at him but didn't respond, so he asked, "How's the philosophy club meeting going?"

"Fine," she replied in a brisk tone. "Ella asked me to grab another box of crackers for our cheese board."

"Here, I'll get it," he said, retrieving a box from the cabinet and handing it to her.

"Thanks," Marni grumbled.

"You'll be at Ella's birthday party next week, right?"

"Yeah."

"It's just what Ella wanted: dinner with our closest friends. My parents are watching the kids," Finn said. "The tapas restaurant we're going to is great. I reserved a dimly lit private room with lots of ambiance, and they're decorating the table with an ornate tablecloth, flowers, boatloads of candles, and these little gold-colored globes I found as take-home gifts. Don't tell Ella. I wanted to surprise her and make it special the way she always does."

She snorted loudly, turning to walk away.

"Marni, is everything okay?" he asked. "Have I done something to offend you?"

She swiveled around on her heel and stared daggers at him. "I've been trying very hard to bite my tongue. I always knew you were too good to be true. I let my skepticism go and believed you actually loved Ella for who she is and that you made her happy. I was totally on Team Finn. Now you fucking do this. I can't believe you, after how she's followed you around the world to film set after film set, supporting your career, taking care of your children, putting her own work aside." She rolled her eyes. "I should have known all along. You're just like all the rest."

He furrowed his brow in confusion. "I have no clue what you're talking about."

"The fellowship. The University of Cambridge. I guess to you it's nothing in comparison to making millions of dollars for a movie, but for a philosopher, it's the most prestigious fellowship in the world. It's a once-in-a-lifetime opportunity. The odds of actually getting it out of the hundreds who apply are unfathomable."

"Are you saying Ella was invited to the University of Cambridge?"

Marni stood silently for a moment. She huffed and said, "Wow, I guess she didn't tell you. I just assumed . . ."

"Please just tell me what's going on," Finn implored her.

"Ella received a fellowship for the upcoming spring semester. It's to finish her philosophical treatise on love, which you know she's been writing for years. It comes with an award, an office, the opportunity to deliver a series of lectures, and lots of other perks. It's basically the most coveted opportunity for philosophers the world over, not to mention a real chance to complete the most important book of her career."

He shook his head, trying to process what he was hearing. "That's amazing. She never said a thing about this to me. Maybe she's not interested?"

"Finn, this didn't fall out of the sky. She applied for it more than six months ago."

"I don't understand. I . . ."

"She said that she turned it down because you have some film project and that it's the last chance for you to take location jobs outside of summers since Betty starts school in the fall, and you agreed you'd always keep your family together."

Finn inhaled deeply and ran a hand through his hair. "I honestly had no idea."

"I can see that," Marni said. "Listen, I'm sorry I jumped down your throat. I just assumed . . ."

"It's fine. Please don't mention this to Ella."

Marni nodded.

THE EVENING OF ELLA'S BIRTHDAY DINNER, she emerged from the bathroom wearing a lavender silk dress, her lips shimmering, an iridescent shine on her cheeks, and her wild mane flowing freely. "Wow! You are absolutely stunning," Finn said, kissing her softly.

She smiled. "I guess happiness does that to a person."

He took her hand and cupped her cheek. "Are you happy, Ella? Are you truly happy?"

"Well, of course, silly. I have you."

Finn smiled. "You do have me. Always. You know that, right?"

"Yes," Ella said, smiling. "What's going on with you?"

"Nothing. I love you so much. Sometimes I just want to be sure you know that."

"I do," she replied.

He kissed her forehead. "Shall we go, sweetheart?"

ELLA COULDN'T STOP SMILING AS SHE looked at Finn across the beautifully set, candlelit table, surrounded by a dozen of their closest friends, all happily chatting. Waiters cleared the dinner dishes and refilled everyone's water and champagne glasses.

Lauren picked up her globe, turned to Ella, and said, "We're doing it. We're finally taking that trip to Paris. We leave tomorrow for a two-week trip."

"Oh, wow! That's wonderful. Are you bringing Sophie?"

Lauren shook her head. "My folks are watching her."

"Actually, we have some news, but we don't want to steal the spotlight," Michael said.

"Don't be silly. Tell us. Hey, everyone," Ella said. "Michael and Lauren have news to share." She turned to Michael. "Go on."

He put his arm around Lauren and announced, "We got married last weekend. We're going to Paris on our honeymoon."

"Oh my goodness. Congratulations!" Ella exclaimed.

"Wow! That's awesome. Congratulations," Finn said, holding up his glass. "It's about fucking time."

Their friends laughed and raised their glasses. There was a hearty chorus of "Cheers" and "Congratulations."

"We went to city hall. It was just us and Sophie. We wanted to keep it private," Lauren explained.

"It sounds lovely. I'm so happy for you both," Ella said.

"I owe you one, Ella," Michael said. "The things you said to me in Sweden helped me find my way back to Lauren, my true love, my better half."

Lauren blushed.

"You two are a great couple. What the hell took you so long?" Finn asked.

"Honestly, I was scared shitless of commitment, of marriage. I thought it would stifle me or make my world smaller somehow," Michael said. "A couple of months ago, Sophie asked me why her mom and I weren't married, and I couldn't think of a good answer. The question stuck in my mind. I replayed the years I spent without them and then the last several years with them, and it was suddenly clear as day. Lauren brings out the best in me. She makes me more of what I can be, not less." He leaned over and kissed her cheek. He looked back at Finn and continued, "It's like you and Ella. She wasn't exactly the settling-down type either. I figured that if marriage could be so good for you, we should give it a shot too. I even sold my condo."

"We're thrilled for you," Finn said. He looked at Lauren and jokingly added, "Michael is definitely getting the better end of the deal. We'd tell you you're too good for him, but you already know it. Don't take any of his shit. Keep him on a tight leash, and if you need me to corral him, say the word."

Lauren and Michael both laughed.

Just then, a waiter walked in carrying an enormous blueberry pie with a candle in the center. Ella gasped when she saw it. Everyone began singing "Happy Birthday." When they finished, someone yelled, "Make a wish!"

Ella glanced around the table, but her eyes lingered on Finn. She took a deep breath and blew out the candle.

Everyone clapped. The waiter took the pie back to the kitchen to prepare servings. Ella looked at Finn and said, "I can't believe you got blueberry pie. Thank you."

He smiled, rose, and held up his glass. "I'd like to say a few words about my beautiful wife on the anniversary of her birth." Everyone turned to him. "Ella is truly magnificent in every way. She's funny, smart, generous, kind, and damn sexy. I was bowled over the moment I met her. Fell in love with her so quickly, so deeply. Every day since, that love has grown. Hell, I still blush every time she walks into a room." Ella smiled, her eyes becoming misty. "She's my partner in everything. My lover, my best friend, my confidant, my family, my co-parent. God, she's the most extraordinary mother." Finn stopped to just stare at her with unadulterated love. "The words don't exist to adequately capture what a privilege and joy it's been going through two pregnancies with her, or the immense awe and gratitude I've felt watching her bring our girls into the world. They are so lucky to have her. She's so patient, creative, and loving. I know she's the best parent they could ever have because she sees them and loves them for exactly who they are. I love them because they're little pieces of her." Ella could no longer hold back the tears, which began falling down her cheeks. Lauren handed her a tissue.

Ella sniffled and smiled at Finn through her tears. "And as if that's not impressive enough," Finn said, "she's also one of the premier philosophers of her generation, as most recently evidenced by her acceptance as Fellow to the University of Cambridge, the most coveted award of its kind." Ella's eyes widened with surprise as everyone clapped. She tried to choke back her tears as she and Finn gazed into each other's eyes.

When everyone settled down, Finn continued. "So, we won't be around this spring because we're going to England. I've rented us a little two-bedroom, thatched-roof cottage in the countryside near the university. I'll be taking care of our girls while Ella finishes her masterpiece about love. And if Ella is game, we'll continue on to our home in France for the summer, where she can keep writing and the girls and I can roll around in the grass. If you'll all please raise your glasses, here's a toast to my spectacular wife, the woman I worship and adore, the one and only love of my life. To Ella."

"To Ella!" they all repeated.

Waiters scurried into the room, serving everyone hearty slices of blueberry pie topped with dollops of whipped cream, while Finn made his way over to his bride. She pulled him into the corner, tears streaming down her face. He gently wiped them away and rested his hands on her cheeks. She could hardly speak. Eventually, in a faint voice, she asked, "How . . ."

"Marni told me. She thought I knew. I called the university, and they said it wasn't too late to accept the offer."

"I can't believe you did that."

"I'm so proud of you, Ella," Finn said. "You are extraordinary. Why didn't you tell me?"

"I didn't want you to have to choose."

"Oh, sweetheart. Don't you remember? I already did. I choose you. I choose us. Always."

CHAPTER 20

Ella slipped into the cottage after dark and heard laughter coming from the girls' room. She stood in the small arched doorway and watched Finn lying in one of the twin beds, reading their favorite Cinderella book. Betty was curled up on one side, and Georgia was snug in the crook of his arm on the other side, sucking her thumb. He noticed her and they exchanged a smile. He turned the page and read, "Perhaps the greatest risk any of us will ever take is to be seen as we really are." Ella stood watching them until Finn read the last line: "They lived happily ever after."

He closed the book, and Georgia pulled her thumb out of her mouth and said, "Again."

"Now it's time for you two princesses to go to sleep," he said, running his hand over her wispy blonde ringlets. "We'll read it again tomorrow." He picked Georgia up and carried her to her bed. "Sweet dreams, little peach." Then he tucked Betty under the covers and said, "You have sweet dreams too, my angel."

Ella strolled over and kissed each girl on her forehead.

Finn switched off the light, and he and Ella ambled to their cozy living room and plopped down on the couch, toys strewn everywhere.

"Hi, love," she said, giving him a soft kiss. "That was a sweet sight. I'll never be able to explain how my heart overflows when I see you that way with our children, so tender, close, and loving." She shook her head. "It's very special."

He kissed the tip of her nose. "You happened to catch a rare quiet moment."

"How did things go today?" she asked.

"The cat threw up. Georgia touched it, of course, and then she tripped on Betty, toppling her over. Betty got some in her hair and totally freaked out. So, I had to give everyone a bath. Then the girls had a knock-down, drag-out fight over a toy that ended with Georgia in tears. We regrouped in the afternoon and did a potato printing art project. Naturally, Betty took great care selecting her colors and crafting her composition. Georgia mixed all her paints together and kept stamping one image over another, so it just looks like a big splotch of brown poo, but she had a ball and thought it was hysterical." Ella giggled. "Their masterpieces are on the refrigerator. If you're hungry, there's some leftovers from dinner. The chicken is dry, the potatoes are lumpy, and the peas are mushy."

"It sounds delicious," she said with a laugh.

"I'm hopeless in the kitchen," Finn lamented with a shrug.

"Did you follow Joyce's recipe?"

"Yeah, and I FaceTimed her twice. She agrees that I'm hopeless."

Ella giggled again.

"Fortunately, if you let them dunk it in applesauce, the girls will eat just about anything," he said.

"So, in other words, it was a rough day?" she asked.

He shook his head. "It was a perfect day." He ran his finger along her hairline and gave her a kiss. "What about you, baby?"

"Marni texted me. She's signed up for some Internet dating site."

"Wow," Finn said, raising his eyebrows in surprise.

"I know, shocked the hell out of me too. After the toast you made at my birthday party, she said she couldn't help but wonder if there is something to this whole romantic love thing after all. She did add that there's no reality in which she'll be donning a white dress or wearing 'mosquito netting' around her face."

He laughed. "How's the book coming?"

"It's almost done. I finally figured out how to answer my big question: When we love so deeply, where do we end and where does the other begin?"

"Tell me."

"It all came back to something Albie and I talked about," Ella said. "Do you remember that time in Sweden when you all had a day off from filming, so we took a hike in the forest?"

He nodded. "You and Albie trailed behind the rest of the group."

"I was telling him how being in nature makes me feel so small, but also like I'm part of something bigger, and that makes me feel truly alive. He said that the same could be said of love. He said, 'When you fall in love, it suddenly isn't all about you anymore, and that's such a relief. You're forced to let go, to realize you're part of something bigger. You come to understand that what you share, and indeed that the other person, is more important than you are.' That freaked me out."

"I have no doubt," Finn said with a laugh.

She playfully patted his chest. "I asked Albie if that was dangerous, that if by allowing someone else to become your world, you lose yourself. He said that if the relationship is right, you become their world too, and that ultimately, the safety of that allows you to become more of yourself, not less."

"He sure was smart about life," he said, smiling.

"In the forest that day, the trees were so tall we could hardly see where they ended and where the sky began." Ella stopped and smiled. "That's how it is when we truly love. We're each still who we are, but the borders between us become harder to discern, and soon, we let go and stop looking for them." She ran her finger down his face. "There's so much beauty in that magical space where the trees touch the sky."

"Seems like you had the answer all along."

"Only thanks to the people under this roof, and one who's watching over us from above."

Finn planted a lingering kiss on her mouth. "Today, when it was total mayhem and I was cleaning up cat puke and Betty and Georgia were tripping all over each other in this little place, it occurred to me that we finally have everything we ever wanted."

"Well, not quite everything."

"What's missing, my love?" he asked.

"A little boy."

EPILOGUE

April 7   *Entertainment News Report*

Yesterday, legendary actor Finn Forrester and his wife, Gabriella Sinclair Forrester, welcomed their third child, the couple's first son. We're told the six-and-a-half-pound boy and his mother are both doing well. The world has been captivated by this fairy-tale romance since their showstopping engagement on the red carpet in Cannes. The couple originally met on location for Jean Mercier's film *Celebration*, for which Forrester won the Oscar for Best Actor.

Hollywood fans will be delighted to learn that the pair have named their son Albert Sinclair Forrester. In a brief statement released to the press, they announced, "We have named our son after our dear friend Albie Hughes, who taught us how to live and love with gusto." We reached out to the late actor's widow, Margaret Hughes, who said, "My darling Albie would be deeply touched by this loveliest of honors."

Other stars were quick to add their congratulations. Willow Barnes tweeted, "Aww . . . you have the most beautiful family ever," followed by a string of heart, smiley face, and balloon emojis. Charlotte Reed commented, "Congratulations! Love seeing your family grow. Will never forget our summer together when your romance began," and Michael Hennesey commented, "There's a bottle of bourbon and a case of smokes coming your way. Albie would have approved." On his way to a film screening, Mercier was asked what he thought about the latest baby news. The normally off-color filmmaker smiled and said, "I am very happy for my friends and their beautiful family. They make me believe that all is not lost."

It has already been a busy year for the couple. They brought their brood to England, where Sinclair was Philosophy Fellow at the University of Cambridge, and then summered in their home in France before jetting to Vancouver where Forrester shot his latest film. Sinclair's recent book, dedicated to her husband and simply titled, *Love*, received critical acclaim the world over and has been touted as "one of the most important contemporary philosophy texts of our time." She's now signed a publishing deal to write a series of fairy-tale books inspired by her children and espousing her philosophical views on love. We're told the couple is looking forward to spending some time at home before packing up their family to head to an undisclosed location, where Forrester is scheduled to star in his second Mercier film.

ACKNOWLEDGMENTS

Thank you to the entire team at She Writes Press, especially Brooke Warner and Shannon Green. I'm incredibly grateful for your unfailing support. I also extended a spirited thank-you to Crystal Patriarche and everyone at BookSparks for helping readers find this book. Thank you to the early reviewers for your generous endorsements. Sincere appreciation to Shalen Lowell, world-class assistant and spiritual bodyguard. Heartfelt thanks to Celine Boyle for your invaluable feedback. Thank you to Clear Voice Editing for the always phenomenal copyediting services. Liza Talusan and the Saturday Writing Team—thank you for building such a supportive community and allowing me to be a part of it. To my social media community and colleagues, thank you boundlessly for your support. My deep gratitude to my friends, especially Vanessa Alssid, Melissa Anyiwo, Sandra Faulkner, Ally Field, Jessica Smartt Gullion, Pamela Martin, Laurel Richardson, Xan Nowakowski, Mr. Barry Shuman, Eve Spangler, and J. E. Sumerau. As always, my love to my family. Madeline Leavy-Rosen, you are my light. Mark Robins, you're the best spouse in the world. Thank you for all that words cannot capture.

ABOUT THE AUTHOR

PATRICIA LEAVY, PHD, is a best-selling author. She has published over forty books, earning commercial and critical success in both nonfiction and fiction, and her work has been translated into numerous languages. Over the course of her career, she has also served as series creator and editor for ten book series, and she cofounded *Art/Research International: A Transdisciplinary Journal*. She has received over one hundred book awards. *The Location Shoot* won a Literary Titan Gold Book Award for Fiction. She has also received career awards from the New England Sociological Association, the American Creativity Association, the American Educational Research Association, the International Congress of Qualitative Inquiry, and the National Art Education Association. In 2016, Mogul, a global women's empowerment network, named her an "Influencer." In 2018, the National Women's Hall of Fame honored her, and SUNY New Paltz established the "Patricia Leavy Award for Art and Social Justice." Please visit www.patricialeavy.com for more information.

Author photo © Mark Robins

Looking for your next great read?

We can help!

Visit www.shewritespress.com/next-read
or scan the QR code below for a list
of our recommended titles.

She Writes Press is an award-winning
independent publishing company founded to
serve women writers everywhere.